The TRUE Definition of NEVA BEANE

The TRUE Definition of NEVA BEANE

CHRISTINE KENDALL

Scholastic Press / New York

Library of Congress Cataloging-in-Publication Data available

ISBN 978-1-338-32489-1

1 2020

Printed in the U.S.A.   23
First edition, September 2020

Book design by Maeve Norton

For everyone who dares to prance

Our deepest fear is not that we are inadequate.
Our deepest fear is that we are powerful
beyond measure.

—Marianne Williamson

Chapter One

CUPS

n. 1. small, bowl-shaped containers for drinking from, typically having a handle *2.* the two parts of a bra shaped to contain or support the breasts

Nana hates Show Your Secret. You know the store I'm talking about. The one that sells underwear. Oh, excuse me. Lingerie. *I feel diminished every time I walk past their window.* That's Nana. It's like she just has to make that point whenever she can. All I can say is it's a good thing we don't live in Center City so she doesn't have to pass by their store very often. She gets mad enough as it is when we're waiting for the bus on Spruce Street and here comes one with underwear ads splashed all over the sides. *See, this is why I prefer the trolley.* She says it in a low frosty voice, just loud enough so all the people standing close to us can hear. That is not the way I want to represent.

My nana's right about a lot of things, but I guess she hasn't noticed the trolley has ads too. They're usually about health care or some other boring thing like that, though. I don't think there's any way of stopping her from complaining, but I wish Nana wouldn't always try to speak for me. I'm twelve years old, I just started wearing a bra, I am going to look at those ads.

Why? That's what I've been trying to figure out. It's got something to do with having breasts; Michelle Overton, the new girl on our block; and being left with my grand-parents while my mama and daddy traipse across Europe on their music tour. *Traipse.* That's a funny word. It means to walk around casually. Kind of like what some older kids do on Friday nights when they're out on Baltimore Avenue looking for a party.

Well, it's not really like that. My parents are working. That's why they left me at home with Granddad; Nana; my brother, Clayton; and my words.

I'm into words like some kids are into music or basket-ball. The way I see it, everybody's got something unique to them. Something that makes them interesting or weird.

So . . . it's probably good to stop right here and say which one of those words describes me. Interesting, weird. Interesting, weird. I'd say I'm much closer to interesting 'cause I question things. Everything. I don't let anything slide. It's like I have a dictionary or an encyclopedia inside my head that I'm always riffling through.

I look words up in a real dictionary too. I have a big one that Mama gave me a long time ago. *Merriam-Webster's Collegiate Dictionary*. I use it to figure out what words really mean, but sometimes words and phrases have double meanings. *A woman without a fragrance is a woman without a future.* A salesclerk said that to me and Nana yesterday when we were walking through Macy's. Nana snatched me away so fast she almost tore my arm off. I knew she wasn't mad at me, though. She was, how would they say it on TV? Overcome by the circumstance. Like the time I told Kira Reynolds off for making fun of the gap between my friend Jamila's teeth.

Jamila's mama's African American, like me, and her *paapa*, her word for daddy, is from Ghana. Jamila Akosua Mensah. My girl is beautiful inside and out. *Ahoufɜ*. That's how you say "beautiful" in Twi. That's one of the languages they speak in Ghana.

Me and Jamila start off every summer morning in the same way. We sit on our front porch and figure out what we feel like doing that day. Now, if my mama wasn't in

Amsterdam (that's in Holland) I'd be with her, but I'm not. She's not here, that is. So I'm not with her.

"Isn't it time to pick the berries?" Jamila asks. The raspberries in the front yard garden of our three-story Victorian house are in bloom and their little red heads peek out from prickly green leaves. They've been like that for a few days already. Jamila grins when she asks the question, and I see the dimple in her right cheek. That's how I know she wants to do some gardening. *Get her hands in the dirt*, as Nana would say. I'm thinking about how much I like wearing my new bra so it takes me a little minute to focus on the garden, although the tomato, zucchini, and cucumber plants look peaceful in the early-morning light.

"Huh, Neva," Jamila says, poking me in my side. "The garden. Ask your nana if I can help out."

That's Jamila. She likes eating the stuff we grow and she's willing to work for it too. She doesn't try to take advantage of other people like some folks do. I give her a playful slap on the shoulder to show my appreciation.

Across the street Michelle Overton steps out in a bikini. A sarong is knotted at her waist so we can't see her butt but her breasts are on full display in her demi-cup halter top. She's two years older than us but even two years

4

cannot account for all that. She's *hot and happening* like that ad I saw on the casino bus last week.

Now, I'm not trying to say I understand why anybody would waste their money gambling, but Granddad says some people are addicted to it. That means they'd go to the casino no matter what so I don't see why the people who run the casinos have to put the ads with women with hardly any clothes on flat out on the side of their bus. I guess they want to make sure nobody slips away to put their money in the bank or do something else good with it, like donate to charity.

Jamila leans over the porch railing and looks down at the beetles in our garden. Me? I can't stop looking at Michelle. How can she prance around the neighborhood like that? Whenever Jamila and I walk the four blocks over to the swim club we wear shorts and T-shirts over our bathing suits.

"These raspberries need to be picked," says Jamila, holding her braids to one side. Her auntie runs an African braiding salon up on Fifty-Second Street so Jamila's hair always looks good. "That's the best way to get rid of beetles."

"How do you know?" I ask, but my eyes are still locked tight on Michelle. For real. She doesn't just walk down her front steps. Uh-uh. Miss Thang descends like a goddess. Her light brown skin is tanned to a rich, dark sheen. That girl is spending a lot of time at the swim club. She smiles at me and Jamila but she doesn't say anything.

Jamila scoots off the porch down onto our front steps. She reaches way over into the garden and picks up one of the beetles. "Cute, isn't it?"

Cute is totally the wrong word for this moment. We're cute. Michelle's something else.

Jamila finds a twig by the side of the steps and sticks it down in the raspberry patch. She waits until a few beetles climb up on it before raising the twig to eye level.

"I just want a closer look," she says, cupping her free hand around the twig.

I'm peeking down the front of my WEST PHILLY T-shirt. My bra doesn't have demi-cups and Nana would rather *walk twenty miles on bad backcountry road* (another one of her sayings) before she'd let me get one. Even if I could fill it.

"I can see you're distracted," Jamila says without turning around.

What? She's got eyes in the back of her head like old people?

My girl faces me and coaxes her dimple out again, except this time it doesn't work. Something's changed.

Jamila's grin fades and she puts the twig back down in the garden. "Who cares about Michelle?" she says. "I have other things to worry about."

I care about Michelle and my brother, Clayton, does too. He's sixteen and he's a lifeguard at the swim club. He comes and goes as he pleases. Well, he tries to. He and Granddad have been going at it about his music, his curfew, his friends. Basically everything but especially politics or "social activism" as Clay calls it. He feels bad whenever we pass homeless people standing outside Mariposa Food Co-op. You can see it in his eyes. He can't just walk by them like they don't exist like other so-called neighbors do. And he's worried about all the people in our neighborhood who came here from other countries— Vietnam, Liberia, Ethiopia. We have it all right here. And we have Michelle too. Michelle.

It's not that I can't, but I don't put my thoughts about Michelle and Clayton into words. Something about that scares me. Like being without Mama and Daddy this summer.

There's an awkward silence between me and Jamila and she's the one to break it.

"Okay, Neva," she says, standing up. "Talk to you later."

I lower my eyes as if I'm fascinated by something in the garden. I don't say anything to stop Jamila from leaving because something's pulling me back into the house. Something having to do with Michelle Overton and my profile. I need to see it again. My profile, that is. I need to check it out. I've only done this about eight million times this past week since I got my bra.

I don't hear anybody upstairs so the coast must be clear. The problem is the mirror in my room is too small. So is the mirror in the bathroom. I need a bigger mirror to really check everything out so I go into my grandparents' bedroom to the biggest mirror in the house.

I stand in front of my grandparents' bureau and smile. I love the way I look, starting with my new do, my twists, so I gently pat my hair before turning to the side to admire my body. I lift my lavender T-shirt so I can see the glorious white cotton status symbol against my walnut flesh.

Yeah, I'm all that. Michelle Overton might be going to high school, but she's got nothing on me. I admire myself from the front, from the back, from the left, and from the right. I do this over and over again until I am dizzy.

I don't know how long I have been posing when the door to my grandparents' bathroom flies open and Clayton falls out. He screeches, screams, shrieks, hollers, and howls his way across the room. Clay is laughing so hard he can hardly walk. Do you hear what I'm saying?

His eyes are sealed shut as he gasps for air, struggling to regain control of his heaving shoulders. He falls to his knees and bangs his right fist on the floor like a judge trying to keep order in his court. He staggers to his feet and roars past me without saying a word.

Chapter Two

AJAR

adj., adv. neither entirely open nor entirely shut; partly open: *The door was ajar.*

I pull down my shirt and stare at the half-open bathroom door. I walk over to it and grab the doorknob. I pull the door open all the way then I close it, open close, open close, as if the door is a giant eraser that will remove all traces of the last three minutes.

I. Don't. Know. What. Happened. Why didn't I check to see if anybody was in the bathroom? Why wasn't I more careful?

I wish I could jump out the window, or crash through the roof. I need to do something so I run back to my room and call Mama. I need to hear her voice. Please, please answer . . .

No luck.

My mind races as I call Jamila. Prancing. Is that what I was doing? Up until this morning I thought only horses pranced but then I saw Michelle and then I wanted to prance too but I only wanted to do it for myself but then my newsy brother saw me and now I'm afraid to leave my room.

How did this happen?

I can't reach Jamila either. Where is she? My hand goes up to play with my hair. *Twisting my twists*, Granddad calls it. Something I have a bad habit of doing when I'm upset but now I'm beyond upset. I feel ajar. I know that word from reading Nana's psychology magazines, but I've never used it before. I never had to because I never felt exposed like this. I mean, my stomach's flipping and flopping like it did when I got sick at the carnival. My neck is stiffening up like it does before I get a headache and I definitely don't want to go there.

If Mama, the best songwriter in the world, were here she'd say, *Sing a song to yourself. Something sweet, something soothing.* I open my mouth but nothing comes out.

Clay saw me prancing. I lie down on my bed and curl up in a tight little ball like a box turtle retreating back into its shell.

Chapter Three

VULNERABLE

adj. 1. susceptible to physical or emotional attack or harm: *We were in a vulnerable position. 2.* open to moral attack or criticism

"Bring your dirty clothes down." It's Nana shouting from the bottom of the narrow back stairs that run from the kitchen to the second floor of our house. She doesn't like to make too many trips up and down. Hard on her knees, she says. All I know is I can't face Clay. Not now. Maybe not ever. He's probably still laughing.

"Neva, do you hear me, girl?" Nana calls up the stairs again.

I could say I don't feel good but I don't want to make her climb up here. It wouldn't be a total lie, though. I still have a tingling. No, that's not it. I still have a clawing feeling in my chest and I really, really don't want to see Clay.

If he sees me he'll start laughing again and Nana will want to know why. And I know my brother; he won't be able to hold it in. He'll tell her about me and the mirror.

I raise myself up onto my elbows and listen for the usual signs of Clay, music or footsteps above my head, but there are no sounds of life coming from his attic room. The one place in the house where my grandparents never go. What is it Granddad says? *A man needs his privacy.* Whatever that means.

I pick up the dirty clothes hamper and hold it in front of me like a shield. Just in case. It's a babyish thing to do. I know. But if I run into Clay I'll dump the hamper on his head if he even cracks a smile. Suffocation by socks. Sounds like one of those old movies Granddad likes to watch like *The Brother from Another Planet.* He calls them classic. Right. That's just an old-school word for something that nobody under thirty is interested in. I tiptoe down the winding stairs, clutching the hamper so tight I can hear the wicker creaking.

Nana's in the laundry room behind the kitchen, leaning on the spinning washing machine. I look outside and marvel at how laundry day turns our backyard into a maze of dancing shapes and colors as pajamas, sheets, and socks flap in the breeze. We have a clothes dryer but my grandmother only uses it in the wintertime or if it's raining.

"I almost forgot about your stuff," she says. "But then the only bras I saw were mine." She smiles at me in a funny just-between-us-girls kind of way. "I knew that wasn't right."

I love my nana even though she's really, really old-fashioned. Nobody has to look that word up, right? Except I do because I want to know all about this word that I'm going to have to deal with all summer.

Old-fashioned: favoring traditional and usually restrictive styles, ideas, or customs

I knew that part already but I didn't know there's a drink made with whiskey called an old-fashioned. I'll probably never get to taste it because there's hardly any drinking of alcohol in our house. That's why everybody was surprised when Granddad brought home a bottle of champagne. The cork shot halfway across the room when he opened it and I had to duck down behind my chair to avoid getting hit in the face. Is that what high-backed chairs are for?

That was the night before Mama and Daddy left for Europe. Granddad made a toast, and even me and Clay got a half of a little, little glass of champagne. I thought it would be something special after all I've heard about it. You know, people always have champagne at their wedding receptions, or retirement parties, or bougie family reunions. But, turns out, it wasn't that good. I couldn't stand the bubbles, but Mama's eyes were shining like they do when she sings so I tried not to gag and ruin it for her. Clay looked at me funny and then started complimenting Nana on the special dinner she made so everybody's attention went to her. Clay took the pressure off me just when I needed it. He's good like that . . . most of the time.

Like I said, Nana can be very strict but she can also be very sweet. My parents had to move our whole family in with Nana and Granddad after they lost our old house. That was a long time ago. Back when Mama's and Daddy's music careers were *on the skids*, as Granddad likes to say. But six weeks ago they got invited to replace Ms. G's opening act on her three-month world tour. Paris, Amsterdam, Berlin, and some other places I can't pronounce. Mama singing and Daddy playing his guitar. They couldn't turn it down. I know. They're going to be famous after this, for real. I just wish they could have taken me with them.

I almost tell Nana what happened upstairs but I can't figure out the right way to say it:

Nana, Clay saw me with my T-shirt pulled up.

That's way too vague and it leaves me wide-open for the follow-up question, *Who pulled it up?* Better find another way to say it:

Nana, my brother, Clayton, knows I wear a bra.

Where did that come from? She knows Clayton is my brother so that's not a good start. And then there's the question, *How does he know?* So, how about this:

Clay found me admiring myself in the mirror in your bedroom, Nana.

I like the word *found* because I'm sort of lost right now. But Nana'll want to know what I was doing in her room. What I was doing in her and Granddad's bedroom. Plus, it sounds like I was doing something wrong and I wasn't. I wasn't.

I unload the washer and almost bump into Nana when I turn around. She's so pretty with her dark brown skin and round face. Her body's full and firm. She must have been really hot when she was young 'cause she still has it going on. I'm in good shape if I have her genes. But Clay found me. What he saw was just meant for me . . .

Wait a minute, what was Clay doing in there? Nana said she knew something wasn't right. Was she talking about me or was she talking about Clay? Hmmm. What was Clay doing? Spying on me? He's never done that before. At least, not that I know of.

I think about that as Nana and I step outside and work our way down the clothesline with me handing her wooden clothespins at just the right moment. I'm happy my headache didn't develop so every few steps I bury my face in the clean, dry clothes and breathe in a big whiff of sunshine.

"You don't get that smell when you use the dryer," Nana says. She's right and the fresh fragrance helps me think straight.

"Where's Clay?" I ask.

Nana shrugs. "I don't know. He ran out of here like the house was on fire."

I don't think she'd be so calm if she didn't know where I was. Granddad almost had a fit when I was twenty minutes late coming home from Malcolm X Park last week. But I don't want to get stuck on that right now.

"Was he laughing?"

"Laughing?" Nana looks at me with one eyebrow raised. "Definitely not. He was all plugged into that thing." She holds a red-and-white dish towel up to her face and moves her head from left to right like she's reading from a screen. She's actually pretty funny. "He's keeping a lot of stuff to himself these days. Who knows what's going on with him," she says.

Yeah, who knows what's going on with Clay, or with me for that matter.

Chapter Four

(ANOTHER)
HUMILIATION

n. the state or feeling of having experienced a painful loss of pride, self-respect, or dignity: *She fought back tears of humiliation.*

"Shut up," says Jamila. I've just told her about what happened. She's standing in front of me with her eyes all wide and her bottom lip quivering. "I'd die if anybody saw me doing that."

Jamila's been wearing a bra for months already so she's more used to it. I've never asked her if she's done any prancing, but her response to my confession, folding her arms across her chest and avoiding eye contact, makes me think she has.

She's looking out across her family's cement backyard to the mural painted on the wooden fence. There's no grass in their yard but her mama's made it nice with a little café table; chairs; a white umbrella; and, of course, the red, gold, and green Ghanaian flag. Her daddy's mural of a market day in Accra with people in colorful kente clothes buying and selling things—fruit, plantains, chickens—sets the yard off really nice. Mr. Mensah manages Jamila's auntie's braiding salon, but he's an artist too.

Jamila's perfect for discussing dramatic events like what happened this morning. She understands my humiliation and tries to help me think everything through.

"It's not like Clay's going to tell anybody else," she says. "You're his sister so it's just between you two."

We both remember fast Kira Reynolds who had some pictures taken that she shouldn't have at a sleepover and later found them online. *Fast*, that's Nana's word. I'm a little surprised it rolled off my tongue so easily. I try not to do that. Shame girls, that is. I mean, have you ever heard of a boy who wasn't running somewhere referred to as fast? No. And you probably never will is all I'm saying.

I'm not worried about Clay sharing anything online, but I confess my fear that Clay'll start laughing as soon as he sees me and he'll end up telling everybody what happened. I especially don't want Granddad to know. He doesn't seem to know what to do with me since Mama and Daddy left. He keeps coming up with all these rules that I didn't have before. Like I can't go to a coed sleep-away camp anymore which, by the way, is fine with me. I never really liked it but it feels like he's trying to think up ways to keep me in the house.

"If Clay was smart," says Jamila, "he'd keep this whole thing to himself unless he's prepared to say what he was doing in your grandparents' *master bedroom suite*."

She stresses *master bedroom suite* like it's something you can win on a game show.

Neva Beane, come on down!!! You have a chance to take home this magnificent master bedroom set provided you first cover the lower half of your face with your hands like you just can't believe it's true, and then scream and jump up and down while clasping your hands in front of your chest.

In other words, make yourself look like a natural fool. Something I seem to know how to do without going on TV.

I like Jamila's thinking but I hardly have a moment to consider it before she comes up with another option.

"Or you could tell your grandparents what happened yourself." Her eyes are as big as saucers now. "Then they won't ask Clay why he's laughing and the whole thing will be OLD NEWS." She shouts her last two words because a car playing really loud music comes down the street and we can hear it all the way back here.

"I already tried to tell Nana but I couldn't find the right words." I'm leaning close into Jamila because I don't really want to shout that out.

My girl's eyes narrow. "You couldn't find the right words? Dang."

She thinks for a few seconds and then shrugs her shoulders. "Maybe he'll forget about it?"

"You didn't see him," I say, shaking my head. "He was cracking up. There's no way he's going to forget it anytime soon."

"Wow," says Jamila. "You must have really . . ."

Okay, I know I made it sound like I hate the car with the loud music but it's playing one of Ms. G's songs and me and Jamila start swaying.

". . . put on a show," she says, half smiling.

Now here's where I go wrong. Here's where the trouble starts.

I shouldn't let the music and Jamila's smile egg me on, but I do. I figure Jamila's daddy's at work and her mama's upstairs with her baby brother so I feel free to demonstrate what I did in front of the mirror, without pulling up my T-shirt, of course.

I turn around and stand Jamila's library book up on

the table like it's a mirror and strike a few poses in front of it like I'm onstage. I cup my hands over my breasts and Jamila shrieks.

"No you didn't!"

I throw my head back and hug myself like I'm in a music video. I'm not twerking. Okay? I do not twerk. But let's just say I'm moving my hips and I've got my hands all wrapped around myself so it looks like my hands are somebody else's hands. This is way more than I did in front of the mirror, but this is me and Jamila having fun.

"Oooh, Neva." Jamila's laughing and my eyes are closed and I'm imagining I'm on a beach in Ghana with sand between my toes and the warm sun beating down on my eyelids. I'm feeling really silly and loose and free.

"Neva . . ." Jamila's voice sounds a little different but between the music, the imaginary waves crashing around my feet, and my closed eyes I don't realize how the situation has changed. As in Mrs. Mensah is standing in the doorway.

I don't know how long Jamila's mama has been there but the car drives away taking Ms. G's music and my soul with it. I open my eyes and turn around.

YUP. I just jammed myself again.

Chapter Five

TIGHTROPE

n. 1. a rope or wire stretched tightly high above the ground, on which acrobats perform feats of balancing
v. 1. to walk, move, or proceed on or as on a tightrope: *She tightroped through enemy territory.*

Sometimes I feel like I'm walking a tightrope over a big, big hole. The thing is, I don't know what happens if I fall. What will I fall down into? A big grassy meadow like the Dog Bowl over in Clark Park? Or one of those gigantic sinkholes like the one that tried to eat the Route 34 trolley? I don't really know what a sinkhole is so I look it up.

Sinkhole: a cavity in the ground caused by water erosion

The hole that scares me wasn't caused by erosion. It's in my head but I don't know what caused it or what to do about it. It just feels like I'm not able to be all that I know I can be all the time. It doesn't really make sense.

I used to not worry about anything. I used to just hang out with Mama and help her find the right words for her songs or jump on my bike and race Jamila over to the Woodlands, the big old cemetery around our way, which is kind of like a park. You're not supposed to ride bikes there but sometimes we sneak and do it anyway. It's really not spooky except on Halloween when they decorate the manor house to make the place feel scary.

But now, I don't know what's wrong with me. Why can't I be all of myself anymore?

I can't believe I let Mrs. Mensah see me like that. She must think I'm a hot mess. But at least she's not laughing. Maybe she felt like this once herself. Maybe she was awkward and proud when her breasts first popped out too.

Awkward: causing or feeling embarrassment; not smooth or graceful; ungainly

Proud: feeling deep pleasure or satisfaction as a result of one's own qualities or achievements

I can't look Mrs. Mensah in the eye right now so I look at the bright reds and yellows in the mural on her back fence. The lively market scene convinces me I'm right, but still, she saw me . . .

"You girls want some iced tea?"

Mrs. Mensah's acting like she didn't see anything abnormal. *Abby Normal*, as Granddad would say. He got

26

that from another one of his old movies, *Young Frankenstein*. He's only watched it about twenty-five times.

I don't know if Mrs. Mensah is just being kind or if she's waiting for me to leave so she can tell Jamila I'm not allowed to come over anymore.

I start to say "no thank you" to the iced tea offer but Jamila says "yes" at the exact same moment. I'm still looking at the fence so I can't see Jamila's body language. If I could I'd know if she had a plan or something. Some strategy to get her mama back in the house so I could climb over the fence and make my way past the stray cats, trash cans, and discarded tires in the alley back to the real world. This all feels like a bad dream but I'm awake and it hasn't ended. At least this morning Clay ran out so I didn't have to face him. This is much, much harder.

I reach my right hand up to twist one of my twists but then my ring, the sterling silver heart ring Granddad gave me last Christmas, gets stuck. In my hair. I give my finger a gentle tug but the ring doesn't budge. I can't believe this. I scratch my head with my other fingers like I meant to keep my hand up there anyway, but even that little bit of motion pulls my hair.

I sure can't look at Jamila and her mama now so I drop my head to my right shoulder like I'm stretching out my neck in a yoga class.

Sing a song to yourself. That's what Mama would say. I open my mouth but the only thing that comes out is a warble. I sound like a sick bird.

I've got my left hand in the act now trying to untangle my hair from my ring on my right hand, but I can't do this on my own. Little beads of sweat break out on my forehead. I must look so stupid. So, of course, my phone buzzes. Mama? Her timing is so bad. Why does she choose this moment to return my phone call? Couldn't she have called earlier?

My phone's in my right rear pocket but I can only reach for it with my left hand so I'm totally contorted. Twisted, bent out of shape.

"Girl, need some help?" Is that a giggle I hear in Jamila's voice? I can't worry about it because Mama's on the phone with me.

"Hey, sweetie, what's up?" Her voice comes through loud and clear. "We've been in rehearsals all day."

Jamila's looking at me like I'm an alien 'cause my right hand is still stuck upside my head. "What's with your hair?" Jamila asks. She reaches up and pulls at my hand and I scream which, of course, scares Mama.

"Neva, baby, what's going on?"

"Nothing." That's what I say because how can I explain it all in front of Jamila's mother? I can't tell Mama about prancing in front of Clay and then how swaying to Ms. G's music led me to doubly prancing in front of Mrs. Mensah. I can't tell her that the expensive ring I whined about, begged for, and cried for at Christmastime has turned against me. How can I say that Jamila's standing right next to me fiddling with my hand that's glued to my head all because I don't know what to do with myself?

"Nothing?" says Mama. "Then why are you screaming?"

"We may have to cut it out." Jamila says it all matter-of-fact like she's a doctor diagnosing a patient.

"Cut what?" Mama yells. "And don't tell me 'nothing.'"

Mrs. Mensah steps over. "It's okay, Tracey," she says, bending toward my phone so Mama can hear her. "Her ring is twisted up in her hair but I'll untangle it." She smiles at me. "It happens to me too."

So now I'm standing in the middle of Jamila's backyard with her mama's gentle lavender-scented fingers in my hair. Do all mothers use the same hand lotion? She's very careful not to hurt me and I can feel my hair's grip on my ring loosening up.

"Neva, are you okay?" Mama asks. "I really have to get back inside."

I take a deep breath and fill myself up with the scent of lavender before Mrs. Mensah steps back. That feeling of falling down into a deep hole starts to creep back in. It moves up into my throat and I have to swallow a few times to steady myself.

Mama and I didn't even get to talk. I didn't get to tell her what happened with Clay. How he saw me. How I'm afraid to run into him at home. That's the reason I came over here to Jamila's house. A place where I wouldn't have to hide from anybody, but then I made myself look stupid here too.

"Crisis over," says Mrs. Mensah. My right hand is free, but she holds on to it a little bit longer than necessary. "Now, how about that iced tea?"

"We can get the tea ourselves," says Jamila. "And we might go back over to Neva's to get some fresh mint from her garden. You like mint in your tea. Right, Mama?"

Jamila really is my girl. Not only has she given us a way out so we can go look for Clay, but she's also said the magic word out loud. *Mama.*

I look up at Mrs. Mensah and see her smiling. "Yes," she says, "but don't be too long. I need you back here."

"Bye, Mama," I whisper into the phone, but I know she, Tracey, my mama, has already hung up.

Chapter Six

OFFENSE

n. 1. a thing that constitutes a violation of what is judged to be right or natural: *The outcome is an offense to basic justice. 2.* annoyance or resentment brought about by a perceived insult: *He didn't intend to give offense. 3.* the action of attacking: *The students went on the offense to stop schoolyard bullying.*

Me and Jamila turn the corner onto the street leading up to the swim club. I count three more of those HATE HAS NO HOME HERE signs in people's front yards. That's two more new ones than last week.

Folks in West Philly pull together to support one another. That's why nobody we know feels good about people who came here from other countries having to take sanctuary in churches or developers pushing some families out of the neighborhood. At least that's what

Clay says. He encouraged Granddad and Nana to sign a petition to expand the community garden behind the tennis courts so more people can grow their own food like we do.

"I can't stay away too long," Jamila says, repeating what her mama said before we left their house.

We're right behind a bunch of little kids and their grown-ups staggering along ahead of us. The kids have trouble walking in their flip-flops and keep dropping their towels every few steps so the mamas have to keep stopping to wait for them to catch up. Is that what I have to look forward to if I start babysitting? I like little kids and all, but is that the only job for girls?

"What's your mama need you to do?" I ask Jamila as we step off the curb, into the street to pass the little ones. We're close enough to the swim club that we can hear people squealing and laughing, but those fun sounds don't work their usual magic on me today. I scratch my chest through my T-shirt, hoping maybe that will make the clawing feeling that's still sitting there go away.

"I don't know." Jamila shrugs. We take a few more steps and we're passing through the black wrought iron gate and standing at the swim club's little white turnstile. "My mama's not talking to me about everything like she used to. It feels like she doesn't want me to hear her conversations with *Paapa*."

"Understandable," I say. Mind you, I've never had a boyfriend, much less a husband, but I don't think it's weird you'd want to talk to your husband in private. "I get that," I say, like I'm the big authority on relationships.

Jamila gives me the side-eye, but I'm thinking about Nana and Granddad now. They have private conversations all the time. Mainly about what me and Clay are doing. Then I think about Clay and Michelle. I've seen him talking to her on his phone. I can always tell when he's talking to her and not one of his other friends. He stands differently, sort of hunched over, and he cups the phone with his free hand like he doesn't want anybody else to hear their conversation. When he talks to his boys he stands with his legs spread apart and he usually has one hand folded across his chest like he's The Man.

"My *paapa*'s been working a lot lately. He even got another job," says Jamila, crossing her right arm over her body and holding on to her left elbow. "I hope nothing's wrong between my parents."

"Good morning, young ladies." Mrs. Giles, the swim club manager, smiles at us.

Now that we're here, I'm not quite sure what to do, but

Clay's a lifeguard so this can't be a bad place to start spying on him. I mean, looking for him. I mean, I don't really know what I'm doing right now.

But here's Mrs. Giles. She's Clay's boss and she has a beautiful smile. It lights up her entire face and makes everybody feel good. That's because she's not afraid to open her mouth.

You know how some people try to smile with their lips in a tight little line. It doesn't work. That's not Mrs. Giles. I guess being nice is part of her job but I think it's more than that. It's who she is.

I smile back and look down at my shorts and T-shirt. It's definitely not a bathing suit but Mrs. Giles isn't wearing one either. It hits me that I've never seen her in a bathing suit. She always has on beige khaki Bermuda shorts and a dashiki. Clay says she got the dashiki in Senegal. He says she loves Senegal and that's why she works at the swim club. It reminds her of the capital, Dakar. The club reminds me of Greece. I haven't been to Greece or Senegal but the club's white walls and sky blue floors remind me of pictures I've seen of the Greek isles on the Travel Channel.

We show Mrs. Giles our passes and she waves us through the turnstile so we can sign in. One of her assistants takes her place at the entrance and she turns to go into the girls' locker room. That's when I notice I don't see any panty line. Does that mean Mrs. Giles is wearing a thong? If she were wearing panties we'd see the line. Why am I thinking about this? I can't tell how old Mrs. Giles is but she's probably somewhere between my mama and Nana in age. Did she order her thong online or did she get it from a store? I hope Nana didn't see her switching out of Show Your Secret. I'm staring at Mrs. Giles's disappearing back. It looks like she has a nice body. Wonder why she doesn't wear a bathing suit?

Our first stop at the swim club is usually the girls' locker room, but we're not taking our street clothes off today because we don't have anything on underneath. I know some people swim with nothing on—it's called skinny-dipping—but I can't imagine ever doing that. That's like going topless. Another thing I wouldn't do. I think about the naked bicycle ride we have in Philly every year. Naked. On a bike.

I don't know why I said *we* have it every year. I don't have anything to do with it, but our neighbor Mr. Charles rode in it one year. He told Granddad it helps you feel good about your body. Granddad didn't want Mr. Charles to volunteer with him over at the hospital after that.

Me and Jamila walk past the locker room entrance, past the splashing babies and their babysitters in the kiddie pool, and I freeze. Am I ready to face Clay? What'll I say? Will he start laughing as soon as he sees me?

"What's wrong?" asks Jamila.

Do you see him? I mouth, flattening myself against the white wall so whoever's in the lifeguard's chair at the big pool can't see me. Jamila frowns like she forgot why we came here so I spell out Clay's name in the air. C-L-A-Y. She probably can't read that because she's standing across from me so I whisper his full name, "Clayton."

Jamila backs up to the other wall and cranes her neck as far as she can. She stands on her tippy-toes and inches forward against the wall. Jamila could be a model. Her long legs extending out of her pink shorts look like cinnamon sticks against the white wall. Her neck is long and delicate and she swivels her head like a beautiful bird. I can definitely see her on the cover of *Vogue*.

"Everything all right, girls?"

Mrs. Giles stands between us. Her eyes are twinkling like she just heard a good joke.

"We're ... fine," says Jamila. "Just looking for our friend."

"Who's that?" asks Mrs. Giles. "Maybe I can help."

Jamila looks at me like she doesn't want to give anything away. We should have thought this through before we got here. Poor planning, I know. I don't want Mrs.

Giles to think something's wrong with me so I tell her we're looking for Clay.

"Your brother's my best lifeguard," she says, "but he's not here. He's off on Mondays."

Clay's off on Mondays? I don't think my grandparents know that. My brother leaves the house at the same time every morning as if he's going to work. This brings me back to the concern I didn't want to get bogged down in earlier. Nana and Granddad keep much closer tabs on me than they do on him. I start to twist my hair. Carefully this time. I've just stumbled onto some big-time intelligence. As in secret information with potential. Now I've got something on Clay.

"Oh, thank you," I say. "I forgot about his day off."

There's a big commotion with a lot of people at the turnstiles and Mrs. Giles excuses herself to take care of it, but not before telling us to practice our swimming so she can hire us in a few years.

Me and Jamila walk over to the main pool area and now I'm really sorry we don't have our bathing suits. It's starting to get hot and the water looks so cool. We sit on two lounge chairs in the shade.

"Why are we here again?" asks Jamila. "I mean, what's our goal?"

My girl's asking good questions. I think about that

messed-up moment when Clay came bursting out of my grandparents' bathroom and ask myself if it would be better to just forget about it. You know, put the whole episode, event, catastrophe, whatever you want to call it behind me. I'm still embarrassed about it, though, and the only way I can feel better is to go on the offense. Plus, now there's something else I'd like to know. Where is Clay on Mondays?

Chapter Seven

PRIDE

n. I. the consciousness of one's own dignity: *She swallowed her pride and asked for help.* *2.* a person or thing that is the object or source of a feeling of deep pleasure or satisfaction: *The swimming pool is the pride of the community.* *3.* a group of lions forming a social unit

"I need to know what's up with Clay." That's what I tell Jamila.

"Is that the only reason we're running around in this heat?" She's fanning herself with both hands and looking up at the pastel-blue ceiling of the little pavilion where we're sitting. It has a ceiling fan but that's not really helping with the humidity.

"Well," I say, lying back and closing my eyes. "He hurt my feelings . . . my pride."

"Isn't pride a bad thing . . . sometimes. If it's taken too far?" Jamila's losing steam. I can tell.

Clay saw me during a private moment. That's why I'm upset. I still have a tingling in my chest when I think about it.

I look over at Jamila. "Why didn't your mama ask us what we were doing? You know, earlier."

"I don't know." She shrugs. "Sometimes she's really strict—"

"She's not as bad as my grandparents."

Jamila nods. "But she doesn't try to make anybody feel worse than they already do."

I love Mrs. Mensah. Not only did she give me a graceful exit this morning but she's always around. We lie quietly for a few minutes until some older boys we don't know run and jump into the pool making a really big splash. Jamila sucks her teeth and the lifeguard with the funny-looking sunscreen on his nose blows his whistle and shouts, "No running."

Lifeguard. That could be a fun job. Imagine sitting up there with people looking up to me all day. That's a job with real responsibility, but taking care of somebody's baby is serious too.

I'm thinking about all the things that could go wrong

with a baby when in walks Michelle Overton. *Radiant* is the word that pops into my head when I see her.

Radiant: sending out light; shining or glowing brightly; emanating great joy, love, or health

It's how our neighborhood feels in springtime when all the gardens start to come alive. At least that's how I see Michelle. I can't speak for Jamila, who's checking her phone as if there's nothing more interesting to look at.

"We better get that mint from your garden," she says. "I promised my mama."

She can't be serious. How can we leave now? Michelle in her demi-cups. They're what started this whole mess. I try not to stare but I can't help it.

"Michelle's not the only person with a body, Neva," Jamila says in a flat voice. "Don't forget, Serena Williams, Misty Copeland, Beyoncé, Mrs. Giles . . ."

What? My head is spinning even though I'm lying down. I sit up thinking that might help. Mrs. Giles? How did she get in the same league as Queen Bey? Michelle I can see. I look at Jamila. She really isn't bothered by what she just said. Is that because her hips already have a curve and mine don't?

"I have to go," she says, standing up. "You can stay and, who knows, Michelle's here so Clay may show up."

Michelle's sitting on a lounge chair in the sun and all the boys are checking her out.

"Fifteen more minutes?" I ask.

Jamila shakes her head, but not in a mean way. "I need to get home, but honestly, Neva, you weren't like this before. You're obsessed with Michelle." She puts her hand on my shoulder like a kindly teacher would. "Do you have a crush on her?"

I'm not crushing on anybody. That's not it. But what is true is that something about Michelle stirs things up inside of me. I shake my head no and fall back on my lounger.

"Well, is it still okay if I take some mint from your garden?" Jamila asks.

I nod and for the second time today I watch my friend leave.

I have no idea what I'll do if Clay walks in so I turn over on my side and put my hands under my head like I'm sleeping. Besides Michelle, I only recognize one other person hanging around the pool. Clay's buddy Anton. He's not even fourteen yet, but for some reason my brother lets him hang with him.

I think back to the last few times I've seen Anton. He was really nice when he asked Granddad and Nana if we had any books to donate to Pennsylvania inmates.

Inmates. That's a strange-sounding word. I sort of knew what it meant, but I wasn't totally sure so I looked it up.

Inmate: a person confined to an institution such as a prison or a hospital

Inmates in hospitals?

I asked Clay about it and he said there'd be fewer people in prison if our schools were better. He said some people get into trouble because they don't have any other opportunity. He didn't say anything about inmates in hospitals, though. All I know is Anton almost ripped our screen door off its hinges when Pennsylvania came up with that new law that families can't send books to people in jail. Even I can tell that's messed up, but I haven't talked to anybody about it.

"Feeling okay?"

I recognize the voice but it's coming from behind me so I'm not looking directly at Michelle Overton. I hope my butt doesn't look too big from her perspective.

What? She's walking around so she can see my face? She stands over me and fidgets with her hands. Not something you'd think a goddess would do.

"Hey," she says.

"Hey." I roll over onto my back and pull my cell out of my shorts pocket. I can't believe she's speaking to me so I start scrolling through my messages.

"Where's Jamila?" she says. "I'm used to seeing you two together all the time."

So, Michelle Overton knows me and Jamila exist? I look up at her and see she's got eyeliner and lip gloss on even here at the pool. The makeup makes her look older than she is.

"Jamila's with her mama," I say.

"Oh." There's a pause. "And you're feeling okay?"

"Yup."

Another pause.

"Clay tells me you like to read."

I'm a little surprised about how she jumps right into talking about Clay without any introduction. There's no, *You're Clay's sister aren't you?* or *I met your brother here at the pool.* She just goes for it. She's confident. Something I'm not. Well, I used to be. But I'm not anymore.

"Yeah, I do like to read," I say.

"Read anything good lately?"

"Not really."

Another long pause. I could help her out, but for some reason I don't.

"Are you going to hang out here all day?" Michelle asks.

"Nope."

"Whew." Michelle Overton drops her hands to her

sides. "Clay said you could be tough. He wasn't lying about that . . ."

But I'm not tough. I'm just surprised you want to talk to me. But of course I can't say it. "When did he tell you that?" is what comes out.

"I don't remember." She shrugs. "Maybe when we first moved here."

So, she and Clay have been friends since she moved here six months ago? She says her daddy is a community organizer. She can tell from my face that I don't know what that is so she breaks it down for me.

"My dad brings people together to work on social problems in the community."

"Your daddy's in the right place," I say. "There's a lot going on in this neighborhood. At least, that's what Clay tells me."

"Yup," Michelle says. She doesn't look stuck-up at all. I mean, we, me and Jamila, don't wear bikinis like the one she has on, and our lips aren't moist like hers, but she seems okay.

"How do you like living here?" I ask, sitting up.

"Well, at first it was a little hard to make friends," she says, "but my dad says you can't wait for people to come to you. You have to go to them. And you have to bring something to the table."

"Like food?"

"No," Michelle laughs. "That means you have to have something beneficial to offer the other person. Like friendship or help with something."

I wonder how she and Clay got to be friends and why she and I haven't even had a conversation until now but I don't bring that up.

"I mean," she says, sitting down in the other lounge chair, "I've been meaning to tell you how much I like your hair."

She likes my twists? I sit up straighter.

"But I don't know why I never said anything before today."

"My grandparents aren't really into twists," I say, "but Clay helped me persuade them to let me do it."

"I can see him doing that," she says. "He's strong but sensitive at the same time, you know? A lot of dudes would just play their little sisters off."

A lump rises in my throat as I think about what happened between me and Clay this morning. Wonder what Michelle would think about that? I swallow the lump back down and focus on Michelle again.

"You don't have a big forehead like mine," she says. "You can wear your hair however you want."

Michelle Overton has a big forehead? I look more

closely but I don't see a football field under her bangs. She sees me checking, though.

"I'll show you later," she says, waving her hand. "Just not here. I have my pride."

I can't believe we're laughing about her forehead. I look over at the pool and see Anton looking over at us. Figures. I'm so sure a lot of boys like Michelle but she doesn't seem to care about that right now. She's laughing with me and I start to tell her about all the reading I'm doing this summer. It's all over the place—psychology magazines, a mystery series, and don't forget Mama's songwriting book.

Chapter Eight

HARASSMENT

n. aggressive pressure or intimidation: *The girls faced daily harassment from the construction workers.*

Where are you? It's a message from Nana.

I'm half a block from our house and I see Granddad pacing up and down the sidewalk. It's just my luck that he's out front on the one and only day of my life when Nana doesn't know where I am. Michelle's walking alongside me and I really, really wish she had more clothes on. Like one of Mrs. Giles's dashikis. It's not like she didn't try to cover up. She did put a T-shirt on over her bikini top when we left the swim club but it's wet so it's not helping the situation.

Granddad sees me and Michelle. I wave but he doesn't wave back. We're almost at my house when a loud car—as in loud color, loud music, loud passengers, everything Granddad hates—pulses down the street. This is one of those cars with a sound system that makes the speakers vibrate with every beat. It's a wonder the three guys in it aren't deaf. The driver slows down and hangs so far out his window that his friend in the passenger seat has to grab the steering wheel to keep the car from hitting the curb.

"Yo, beautiful," the driver yells.

His grin is so wide that I can see every single one of his gleaming white teeth and pink gums. He looks Michelle up and down and asks if she's allowed to get phone calls. A really weird way to ask for somebody's phone number if you ask me. Michelle ignores him and looks straight ahead. I'm looking at Granddad and wishing I were somewhere else.

"Check out the little one," the dude in the back seat shouts. "She ain't bad either."

Are they talking about me? I cross my arms over my chest but the boy in the back keeps staring. He doesn't look much older than Clay.

Granddad steps in front of me and Michelle and glares at them.

"Oh, it's like that," the driver laughs. "Catch y'all later after you put Pops to bed."

Granddad turns to me and I don't think I've ever seen him this mad.

"Where have you been?" he says.

Based on how Michelle's dressed and the fact that she's holding a beach towel, I think it's obvious we're coming from the swim club, but Granddad doesn't give me a chance to answer.

"And don't lie to me. Your grandmother tells me Jamila came by here, without you, a while ago."

"Hi, Mr. Robinson," says Michelle. She knows Granddad? She smiles at him but he doesn't smile back. "We were just over at the pool—"

"It's Michelle, right?" Granddad's talking to Michelle but he never takes his eyes off me. "This doesn't concern you."

Michelle gives me the side-eye. "Well . . . bye, Neva," she says, before slowly crossing the street.

I'm looking down at the cracks in the sidewalk trying to figure this all out. It's true I should have let Nana know where I was when I left Jamila's house, but I was only at the swim club for, what, an hour? And it's not like I left the city. I was over at the pool where I'm allowed to go.

Nana comes out on the porch but she doesn't come down the steps to the sidewalk. She leans on the banister and calls to us. "There you are. I was so worried." She sits down in the dark green rattan love seat and waits for us to come to her. "You told me you were going over to Jamila's but then I saw her out here weeding."

"Jamila was weeding?" I ask. "I thought she was just going to take some mint."

"So she left Jamila to hang out?" Why's Granddad talking about me like I'm not standing right here? "She left her friend working in our garden to go mess around with some boys. How long's this been going on?"

"Nothing's going on." I say it a little louder than I mean to but Granddad's trying to build a case against me. A case that's not true at all. "I don't know any boys." That's not true either but you know what I mean.

"Well, they sure looked like they knew your buddy from across the street."

"Who are you talking about, Dexter?" Nana looks at me with her eyebrows drawn together. "Who—"

"Some riffraff—"

"She doesn't know them," I say, shaking my head. I don't know what riffraff is but it doesn't sound good. Why is Granddad making this up? "I never saw those boys before." I'm twisting my hair again now. "Didn't Jamila tell you where I was, Nana?"

"Don't get smart," Granddad snaps. "I'll go over to that pool and check with Mrs. Giles."

"I'm not getting smart. I'm just trying to tell you what happened. Me and Jamila were at the swim club—"

"Jamila and I," says Nana.

"Before you left her to hang with your think-she-grown friend," Granddad adds.

"She left me," I say. "Jamila left me."

"Who is this new friend?" Nana asks again. "Who are you talking about?"

"That girl Clay's been talking to," Granddad says.

So Clay and Michelle are . . .

Nana sighs again. "That fast girl?"

"She's not fast," I say. "She's nice . . . and we were talking about books—"

"What kind of books?" Granddad's eyes bulge all out of his head. "Better not be no *Thirty-Six Shades* . . ."

What are they talking about? I can't stand it anymore. This is double harassment. First from those random fools on the street and now from Granddad. I snatch the screen door open almost as hard as Anton did and run through the vestibule, but I can still hear my grandfather.

"Next thing you know she'll be dressing like her too." I have one foot on the bottom stair when he opens the screen and yells into the house, "That's right, young lady. Go to your room."

I run to my room for the second time today, but this time I slam the door behind me. I lie down on my bed next to my backpack, curl up in a tight little ball, and cry.

Chapter Nine

LONELY

adj. **1.** affected with a depressing feeling of being without company: *Lonely people who have no family.* **2.** destitute of sympathetic or friendly companionship

It's still light when I wake up. You'd think it'd be dark by now after everything that's happened. I look at my cell. Not even five o'clock. I listen hard but there are still no signs of Clay.

I retrieve from my desk the faded red leather-bound dictionary Mama gave me and sit on my bed with it in my lap. Its pages have yellow edges, but I swear I can see the imprint of Mama's index finger on some of them. I look up that word Granddad used earlier.

Riffraff: disreputable or undesirable people

That's a good word for those guys who hit on me and

Michelle. I say it out loud a few times. I don't like the sound of it.

I close the dictionary but still hold it close. Hmmm. Isn't it funny how that word *close* has two different meanings in one sentence? I'm trying to think of other words like that when my phone buzzes.

"Mama?"

"Tonight's crowd was *gezellig*," she says, giggling a little. "That's the Dutch word for 'cozy.' The only thing missing was you and Clay."

What? She's speaking another language now? I ignore that for the moment.

"Can I meet you over there? I promise I won't get in the way."

Mama doesn't respond right away. "I wish you could, sweetie, but this is exhausting work. It wouldn't be a good scene for you."

"I could just stay in the hotel room and read."

"Baby, that wouldn't work. You'd be all alone all the time."

"But I'm all alone here."

"Alone? You have Granddad, and Nana, and Clay right there with you."

"They're not with me, Mama—"

"Neva, hold on a second . . ."

Mama's talking to somebody else. Has she forgotten

what she promised at the airport? I said I'd give the summer a try and she promised to come home if things weren't working out.

I'm still on hold so I look up what she said wouldn't be good for me.

Scene: a place, with the people, objects, and events in it, regarded as having a particular character or making a particular impression

In other words how you represent.

I cradle my phone to my ear but all I hear is the sound of somebody coming up the stairs in our house. It's not Clay because they're not taking the stairs two at a time. Sounds like they have to rest after every few steps.

"Neva," Mama finally says. "Ms. G's expecting me at an after-party so I have to go, but we'll talk again tomorrow. Okay? Love you."

And she's gone.

My stomach feels like it did at the airport when she and Daddy left. All cinched up like it's caught in one of Nana's clothespins.

I remember exactly what Mama said at the Delta/KLM gate: *We can fly home for a weekend if need be.* Why did she say that if she didn't mean it? I don't know what else to do so I kick my backpack hard. It falls off the bed and lands on the floor with a loud thud.

"Neva," Nana calls. She knocks on my door and waits for me to answer. "Are you awake?"

She knocks again but this time opens the door slowly. I'm not mad at her, but first Granddad and now Mama. It's not right.

"Hungry?" she asks.

I shake my head no but don't say anything else.

"Did something happen between you and Jamila today?"

I fold my arms across my chest. "Is it too late for me to go to camp?"

Nana cocks her head to the side.

"Oh," I say. "I forgot I'm not allowed to go."

"Neva . . ." Nana says, reaching for my hand.

She grasps my fingers and I ask why I've been accused of something I didn't do.

"Granddad?" she says. "He's . . . he's just worried about you. And I am too. What happened today? Why didn't you call when you left Jamila's house?"

"We just went to the swim club to look for Clay."

"Clay?" she says, shaking her head. "You're about to worry me to death about Clay."

"Well, do you know where he is?"

Nana's head snaps back. It takes a lot to get her mad

but I can tell she doesn't like my tone. "What is this obsession with Clay?"

"If anybody's obsessed it's Granddad. Why's he making up stories about me?"

"He's afraid for you . . . and how you're growing up."

"I've been growing up for twelve years."

"Neva, watch yourself, now."

"Sorry," I say, lowering my eyes. "Nothing happened between me and Jamila."

"Well you know we're comfortable when you're moving around the neighborhood with her, but not with people we don't know."

"Michelle lives right across the street. You see her all the time."

Nana sighs. "Yes, I see her. How could I not?" Her voice has changed but I know better than to say I don't like it.

"She's already friends with Clay. Why can't I hang with her too?"

"Neva, Granddad told me about those young men in the car—"

"We were just walking down the street. Granddad wants to lock me up because other people are stupid."

"We've talked about this before." Nana holds her right

hand up. "You have to let us know where you are and who you're—"

"It's not like Michelle's hanging out at after-parties or anything."

Nana shakes her head. "I don't know where that came from," she says, "but I'd much rather have you spend your time with Jamila than with Michelle."

"Even though you don't know her."

Nana shakes her head. "I know trouble when I see it."

Chapter Ten

AWE

n. an overwhelming feeling of reverence, admiration, fear, etc., produced by that which is grand, sublime, supremely powerful: *She gazed in awe at the beauty of nature.*

I should have defended Michelle better. That's what I think after Nana leaves. I should have said that wearing makeup and your bathing suit top without a T-shirt doesn't make you a bad person. Except I'm confused about how I feel about Michelle. It's a weird sort of jealous feeling even though I like how I look and I don't really want to look *exactly* like her.

It's not that I don't compare myself to her every time I see her. I do. But I know I'm just as pretty. Just like I know I'm smart. Nobody can tell me I'm not both of those things. It just feels like Michelle's claimed something that I didn't know existed until now. Jamila's right. I didn't used to be like this.

That feeling of falling down into a deep, deep hole starts to creep up again. I felt it when those guys were hitting on me and Michelle out on the street, but I didn't know what to do about it. That was the worst part. If Mama were here she'd know what to do. I wouldn't have to figure everything out all by myself.

I think about some of the signs posted in our neighborhood. *Women have a right to walk in peace.* Maybe we should paint that message on our front steps or stretch a banner across the whole street. Would that make Granddad feel better?

I conjure an image of his face from earlier today and reopen my dictionary to search for just the right word to describe how he looked.

Livid: furiously angry

That's it. I doubt if a banner would make him any less mad. But why's he taking it out on me?

I call Jamila to tell her I now have two people I don't want to see at dinner, Granddad and Clay.

"I'm going to eat dinner in my room," I say. "Off a bed tray."

"Why? Is your head hurting?"

"No, but my granddad accused me of leaving you to go hang out with some boys. Can you believe that?"

"Not at the swim club," she says.

What does that mean, *Not at the swim club*? Does she think I was hanging out with some strange dudes who go around harassing girls or can she just not imagine that happening at our pool? I fill in the details hoping that will clear up the confusion.

"I would've told your grandmother where you were if I had seen her," says Jamila.

"You didn't see her when you were in our garden?"

"Nope. I didn't think anybody was at home."

"That's strange," I say. "She's usually buzzing around the house humming along to the radio." It's no wonder Mama has such a great voice. She got it from Nana.

"I know," says Jamila. "I expected to see her, but then, I expected my *paapa* to be home for dinner tonight but that's not going to happen either . . ."

"Your mama must really be upset."

"That's the funny part," says Jamila. "She doesn't seem that upset about it. I just wish she'd tell me what's going on."

Chapter Eleven

REPRIEVE

n. a cancellation or postponement of an unpleasant situation or punishment: *The students who faced suspension were given a reprieve.*

It must be time for dinner by now. It's been over an hour since I hung up with Jamila and I'm tired of moping around up here in my room. Mama and Daddy had their best performance tonight and now they're out partying. I told them I'd try to make the summer work so I put on the peach V-neck cotton sweater Mama knit for me, secretly hoping that'll make her leave wherever she is, jump on a plane, and magically appear here at home.

That V doesn't need to be too deep, now, Tracey. That's what Granddad said to Mama when he saw the pattern. Like it's a plunging neckline or something. You know, like décolletage, a low neckline.

I open my bedroom door in the way I know how to do without making any noise and listen. Still no sign of Clay. I'm not looking forward to seeing him but I know what to do if he starts laughing when he sees me. I have my ammunition. But hopefully I'll see him before my grandparents do and we can just call a truce.

Truce: an agreement between enemies or opponents to stop fighting or arguing for a certain time

We're not really fighting but my idea is we'll agree that Clay won't talk about me and the mirror and I won't ask what he does on Mondays. At least not in front of my grandparents.

I head down the front stairs and hear somebody setting the table. That's usually my job.

"It's not Sunday, Dexter," Nana calls out from the kitchen. "Don't bother with the good dishes."

Granddad lets out a long sigh. I hear him open the china cabinet and put whatever he took out back in. Granddad setting the table? That's a new one. His footsteps retreat into the kitchen and I hear him opening the cabinets above the sink.

I make my way through the living room and hit the dining room just as he's entering from the kitchen. I always feel like I should stand up straight in our dining room, the most elegant room in our house. Nana and

Granddad are so proud of this room—the parquet floors, the mahogany table, the draperies. I've looked it all up.

Parquet: flooring composed of wooden blocks arranged in a geometric pattern

Mahogany: hard reddish-brown timber from a tropical tree, used for high-quality furniture

This room is my grandparents but it's definitely not me. What kind of a room would I be if I had to choose? I don't know. Probably something lighter and airier. With big windows. Yeah, with really big windows.

Granddad's carrying the everyday dishes and has a yellow dish towel tossed over his shoulder. Not the look of someone who wants to continue a fight.

"I don't know how you girls do this every day," he says, putting the dishes down on the table. "So much back and forth . . ."

I start to say Nana isn't a girl but this isn't the time for that conversation. He's trying to make up for this afternoon. There are many different ways of saying you're sorry.

"You look nice," he continues, with a little hitch in his voice. "Your mama knew what she was doing when she bought that yarn." He smiles and his eyes tell me he really means it. I smile back even though I'm still mad at him. "Food smells good, doesn't it?" He turns toward the kitchen and yells, "Cecily, what time are we eating?"

"As soon as Clay gets home." Nana peeks out from the kitchen. "He should have been here already."

Granddad finishes setting the table and rubs at the brown stains on his shirt. Don't ask me how they got there. I mean, he only set the table. Nana does all the cooking.

"I'm going to change my shirt," he says, heading for the back stairs.

The table's set so there's nothing else to do but wait. I sit in a corner of the living room and leaf through one of Nana's magazines. I don't understand all the words but they talk about interesting stuff like male and female body image. Boys worrying about how they look? Those guys who bothered me and Michelle should have been worried about it. They looked like fools. Who'd want to go out with them?

I gaze over at Clay's photo on the mantel above the fireplace. The one where he's dressed in a toga like a citizen of ancient Rome. It was taken when he got a part in one of Shakespeare's plays. He was the nicest rebellious citizen anybody's ever seen. It was a play but he still had a hard time even acting mean. But you can be a rebel without being mean, right?

Ten minutes go by. No Clay. Granddad comes back downstairs. No Clay. Nana starts to fret about the fish drying out. No Clay. I go outside to get some mint for the lemonade. No Clay. Granddad calls Clay on his cell. No answer.

Is this a reprieve? I don't know how long it's going to last so I stay in the corner.

Granddad calls Clay again. No answer. Nana calls over to the swim club and leaves a message for Mrs. Giles.

"I hope that boy doesn't spoil this evening," says Granddad.

Is that all Granddad's got to worry about? This evening? I'm worried about the whole summer.

I walk over to the dining table and take my usual seat but Nana and Granddad just stand on either side of the room like they're paralyzed.

"Everything looks beautiful, Nana."

Granddad pauses. "Neva's right," he finally says. "Let's start. Clay'll catch up when he gets here."

All the vegetables came from our garden so they should taste really, really good. Except they don't. Where's Clay? He usually lets somebody know if he's going to be late. Nobody's seen or heard from him since he ran out of the house this morning. Nana's worried. Granddad's worried and mad. I'm worried but sort of glad and I don't know what to do with those feelings.

Chapter Twelve

PRESSURE

n. 1. continuous physical force exerted on or against an object by something in contact with it: *The slight extra pressure she applied to his hand.* *2.* the use of persuasion, influence, or intimidation to make someone do something: *The many pressures on girls to worry about their looks.* *3.* slang for high blood pressure, the force of blood pushing against artery walls as it goes through the body

We finish dinner and dessert and still no Clay. Where is he?

Nana gets a return call from Mrs. Giles's assistant, who says she hasn't seen him since yesterday.

"Yesterday?" Granddad sputters when Nana tells him what she just learned. "Where's he been all day? I'm talking about this day. Not no yesterday."

Nana calls Anton, who says he ran into Clay crossing

the playground at Forty-Seventh and Spruce Street this morning.

"Did he say where he was going?" Nana asks. "Was he with anybody?"

Anton says he isn't sure about that but he may have seen Clay with a big bag. Anton's an unhelpful, no, what's that phrase? A reluctant something?

Reluctant witness: someone unwilling or disinclined to say what they have has seen

Anton's definitely a reluctant witness.

Granddad keeps checking his cell to make sure he hasn't missed any message Clay might have sent. "He is officially in trouble now."

Granddad says *officially* like an invisible line has been crossed. If Clay came home even thirty seconds before Granddad's pronouncement would his trouble just be casual? It's dark now. Is that what makes his trouble official?

"I'm about ready to call the police," says Nana.

The POLICE. You don't call the police unless there's a serious problem. I didn't want to see Clay anytime soon but I didn't want anything to happen to him.

"Let's give him until ten o'clock," says Granddad. "It's not ten yet. He's probably just messing around somewhere like that time he went to that party over in

Powelton Village without telling us. Remember that, Cecily?"

Nana nods but she doesn't say anything. She starts to clear the table and I get up to help her when my phone buzzes.

Michelle Overton has my number?

"Hey, Neva," she says. "Clay asked me to give you a call. He's okay. His phone just—"

"Uh, thanks for letting me know," I say as fast as I can. "Bye."

"Is that Clay?" Granddad asks.

"No." I do not want to bring Michelle Overton up with Granddad again so I concentrate on gathering the dirty dishes and avoiding eye contact. That could work, but too bad it doesn't. Granddad's heavy breathing says more than words ever could so I add, "Don't worry, Clay's okay."

"Who told you that?" Granddad says, staring at me like he did this afternoon.

That look scares me so I say the first name that pops into my head. "Jamila. It was Jamila."

"Jamila's out with Clay?" asks Nana. "This late?" She and Granddad are both staring at me now and I wish I hadn't lied. "Does her mama know?" Nana continues.

I shake my head no. I don't know where Jamila is or

what Mrs. Mensah knows but I don't want Nana to call over there.

"It was Michelle," I say. "Michelle said Clay just lost track of the—"

"Michelle Overton?" Granddad's eyes narrow and he sighs like he just can't take any more. "Okay, everybody listen. I'm only saying this once. Clay knows what his curfew is." Granddad taps the face of his watch. "He knows he's supposed to have his BEHIND in this house before ten on weeknights."

"Watch your tone, now, Dexter," says Nana. "It doesn't work on her and it's not good for your pressure."

My hands are full of dishes but I look up and meet Nana's gaze. She's studying me. I look away but I can still feel her eyes on my face. My phone buzzes again so I free up my right hand to pull it out of my pocket and recognize Michelle's number on the screen.

Both of my grandparents are looking at me in a way that says I better tell them who it is.

"Where are they?" asks Granddad. "They better not be out on some date."

Michelle and Clay are dating? I cannot keep my mouth from falling open.

"Take the call," says Granddad. "I want to talk to that girl."

My hands are trying to hold on to too many things—dishes, dessert cups, forks, and spoons. Plus, I still don't want to believe that Clay and Michelle may be into each other like that. It's no wonder I drop my phone and it crashes to the floor, spewing its parts under the dining room table. I feel my face contorting into an ugly grimace.

"It's not the end of the world," Nana says, stunned by my near-tearful reaction to the dead phone. "We'll get you a new one tomorrow."

I hear her but I don't move or say anything right away. My phone was my private connection to Mama. And now the distance between West Philly and Amsterdam just got a million times bigger.

Chapter Thirteen

AFFIRMATION

n. the action or process of affirming something or being affirmed: *He nodded in affirmation.*

Clay's room. I've been in Clay's room so many times. We listen to music and stargaze through his telescope. I don't know why Granddad carries on so much about *a man's room*. Clay's room is cool with its cathedral ceiling and an outside covered balcony where he keeps his telescope. He has a hammock and he sleeps out there sometimes too. He says sleeping outside gives him the space he needs to think about important stuff. Stuff like the kind of world we live in and what we can do to help other people. We can help other people by not spying on them is what I think. What happened this morning still feels bad.

"Geneva," Nana says. "Do you know where Clay is?"

She's calling me by my full, old-fashioned, named-after-my-great-grandmother name now. A sign that things have progressed to a totally different level. I shake my head no.

"Well, maybe we'll find a clue up in his room." Nana walks into the living room and starts up the stairs.

Granddad jumps up and squeezes past her. "Let me go first," he says.

"Dexter, this is no time for your nonsense about *a man's room*." Nana's right on his heels. "I'm going in there."

They're both moving fast and I'm bringing up the rear. We pass my room on the second floor and charge up to the third. Nana's breathing heavily. She's not used to having to go up a second flight of stairs in our house, and it shows.

Granddad opens Clay's door, and it's a big mess inside with clothes all balled up on the floor and a trash can that needs to be dumped. It always looks like this. There's a pair of Jockeys on Clay's bed and Granddad trips all over himself trying to hide it.

"Dexter, please," says Nana. "She's seen that in the laundry."

Nana sits down at Clay's desk and looks at every single

piece of paper, front and back. Pamphlets about the causes of homelessness, flyers requesting book donations for inmates, movie ticket stubs, all of it. I don't think Mama and Daddy ever did anything like this. I make a mental note to never leave anything even halfway incriminating in my room.

Incriminating: making someone appear guilty of a crime or wrongdoing

You definitely should know that word.

Nana opens the top desk drawer and comes across Clay's stash of cards from our parents. I can tell she's not sure what to do. She starts to open one but then puts it back down with the others. They're private in a way all the other stuff isn't.

Granddad looks under Clay's bed and out on the balcony.

"Don't forget the closet," says Nana. Granddad opens the closet door and pushes aside lopsided hangers overflowing with Clay's shirts and pants. Bigger posters about book donations are stacked up against the far wall. TAKE ACTION: OPPOSE THE PENNSYLVANIA DOC'S NEW MAIL AND VISITATION RESTRICTIONS. An image of Anton's clinched fists when he heard about the new book restrictions flashes through my mind. If Clay's fighting against that law I'm glad.

Granddad pushes the posters aside and spies a bunch of red canisters with black tops tucked away in the corner.

"What's this?" he asks, grunting as he squats to examine them more closely. "Police-duty pepper spray?" He picks one up and waves it around in front of his chest.

"Be careful with that," Nana says. "You may accidentally light us up."

"What's Clay doing with this?" Granddad's holding the canister dangerously close to his face. "That's what I want to know."

It's ten minutes to ten and I'm wondering if Nana's going to call the police, although I'm not sure what she'd be calling them for. To come retrieve their pepper spray or to help us find Clay?

I walk out on Clay's balcony so I'm not in the line of any accident Granddad may trigger and I see somebody dart from the sidewalk to the side of the house. It's got to be Clay making his way around to the back door unless, on top of everything else, somebody's breaking in.

Granddad sets the canister down on the far corner of Clay's desk and sits on the bed, watching Nana go through my brother's stuff. He's still fuming but he holds Clay's pillow in his lap like he doesn't want anything to happen to it.

Sort of how I feel, but it's confusing. My brother humiliated me but I still feel protective of him. Like I don't want him to face the full force of my grandparents' wrath. That's much more than plain anger.

Wrath: extreme anger

Clay laughed at me but I can't let him walk into a tornado unprepared.

"I'm going to get some water," I say. Neither of my grandparents respond or even look up so I race down the two flights of stairs as fast as I can. One hand on the banister and one hand on the wall even though Nana hates that. The hand on the wall. She says it leaves a mark.

I make my way through the living room and hit the dining room just as Clay's entering from the kitchen.

"I hope you know they're mad," I say, before noticing how wide his eyes are and the way he's sweating. "Are you okay?"

Clay leans up against the wall. "Where are they?"

"In your room going through your stuff."

"Why are they doing that? I'm not late," he says. "It's just now ten o'clock."

"Nice try," I say. Clay's still breathing hard so I soften my tone and walk over to him. "You missed dinner and nobody knew where you were. Nana called Anton and he said he saw you running across the playground with a big bag this morning." Clay sighs. "They called the swim club and Mrs. Giles's assistant said she hadn't seen you at all today. Plus, Michelle—"

"Michelle Overton . . ." Clay says.

"Yeah, Michelle called to tell me you were all right."

"Did you tell them that?"

"I had to. They think I'm in on whatever's going on with you."

"Nothing's going on with me," says Clay. He makes air quotation marks when he says the words *going on*. Not even I believe that.

"Well, what do you do on Mondays?"

Clay's head jerks back so I tell him what Mrs. Giles told me.

"So, you were spying on me?" he asks.

"Not intentionally," I fib. "Not like what you did to me this morning."

Clay sucks his breath in hard. "Neva, you sound whack," he says. "Mama and Dad told me to take care of you. Nobody said anything about spying."

Clay's statement lingers in the air. His light brown eyes are wide but his eyebrows are drawn together. Mama and Daddy asked him to look out for me?

I look down at the vase of flowers on the dining room table and shrug.

"I was in Nana and Granddad's bathroom getting toothpaste and soap from under their sink to donate to the homeless shelter," says Clay. "Toothpaste and soap." He spits out the word *soap* like it's a dirty thing. "Somebody in this house needs to be doing something," he adds.

I sneak a peek up at my brother. If I didn't know better I'd swear there was smoke coming out of his flared nostrils.

"We have it good, Neva. Granddad bought this house years ago and managed to hang on to it."

"Didn't Nana help him buy it? She worked up until she retired."

Clay nods but he doesn't make the correction out loud. "Lots of folks never had a chance to buy anything. We should help them out."

"But Mama and Daddy lost our old house, remember?"

"Yeah, and look where they are now. In Europe. Plenty of people never get past Fortieth Street."

My brother goes on to tell me about how community organizations don't have enough money to help everybody who needs it. He spends his Mondays collecting donations of clothing and other stuff. Michelle works with the group sometimes too.

"You two have a lot in common," he says. "That's why I gave her your number."

"We do?"

"Yeah, you're both hardheaded in a good way," he says. "I'm surprised you don't know each other."

Hardheaded but good? He hasn't mentioned what he saw me doing this morning at all, but he sees me as determined? I'm either real good at hiding all the questions swirling around in my head or he's just not looking.

"I hung out with Michelle today." That's what comes out. I tell Clay how Michelle came over to make sure I was all right when she saw me all by myself at the swim club. "And then she called tonight."

Clay nods too many times. "She knew I missed dinner and that everybody would be mad."

"But . . . the way you laughed this morning," I say hesitantly, going back to the event I still don't know how to process. The thing that made me feel so bad and messed up my whole day. "You laughed so hard when you saw me . . ."

"I know, I'm sorry," he says, "but you were pretty funny." Clay's eyes sparkle as he chuckles, but I don't say anything so he puts his hand on my shoulder. "Don't worry about it, okay? I just wasn't expecting to see all that when I opened the door . . . somebody so fine." Clay smiles. "You definitely know who you are."

I do know it even though I'm not totally sure of what *it* is. It's not that thing that Michelle has but it's something pretty great. I know. I can feel it. Sometimes.

Clay rambles on about how Mama and Daddy don't want him to be politically active while they're away. *We won't be there to help you out* is what they told Clay. They've had arguments about it and Granddad promised he'd keep Clay *on the straight and narrow* this summer. Now our whole family blames Michelle for Clay's activism.

"As if I don't have my own mind," Clay says. "Like I'm just following some girl."

Clay goes on about how he hadn't meant to miss dinner but there was a late-afternoon rally down at city hall. There were counter-protesters and there was some pushing and shoving.

I'm only half listening because I'm still thinking about what Clay saw this morning. He saw somebody fine. Somebody who doesn't take any stuff. *Fine* is much more than cute and well on the way to beautiful. That's the word I'm going with, but it doesn't really matter what word we use. What's important is we both saw the same thing. We saw me.

My brother wipes the sweat off his forehead with the tip of his T-shirt and walks through the first floor of our house over to the main staircase. He puts one foot on the first step but then leans way back so he can see me standing against the far wall. I strike a pose and Clay beams before flashing the peace sign and taking the stairs two at a time.

Chapter Fourteen

FEAR

n. I. a distressing emotion caused by impending danger, evil, pain, etc., whether the threat is real or imagined *2.* a specific instance of or propensity for such a feeling: *An abnormal fear of heights. 3.* concern or anxiety

Clay isn't a very good liar. I can tell that even though I'm on the second floor and they're still up in his room. He first tells my grandparents he went to the movies with some friends and forgot what time it was. That's not necessarily a bad start but he can't remember the name of the movie he said he just saw. Pit-i-ful. If I were going to use that as an excuse I would have checked the Cinemark website to see what was playing.

"What about the pepper spray?" Granddad asks. "You need all that to keep folks' hands out of your popcorn?"

Clay ignores the questions but switches his story to

87

splitting a pizza with Michelle and some Penn students he said they met on campus. I guess he thinks Granddad will be happy to hear he's researching colleges, but it's summer and there aren't many students around. That excuse would only have worked if he'd said his new college friends were in an orientation program or something. Plus, Clay underestimates the impact Michelle Overton's name has on my grandparents.

"I knew that girl . . . that little missy was in the middle of this," Granddad yells.

"Her name's Mich—"

"I know what her name is. You think I don't know that?"

"She's no good for you, Clay," Nana says. "Nothing good can come from having a girlfriend like that."

"Like what?" Clay's voice is steady. "I don't know what you mean by *girlfriend like that*."

I don't hear anything for a few seconds, but I bet they're all breathing hard and staring at one another.

"She's not my girlfriend, okay?" Clay finally says. "She's a woke sister. Something that's missing from this house."

Granddad tells Clay he didn't invent political struggle and Clay says the world would be a better place if there were more people like Michelle in it. I have to look up *woke* 'cause I'm not exactly sure what it means.

Woke: actively aware of systemic injustices and prejudices

Sounds like Michelle.

My ears perk up again when Clay mentions Anton. "His family's struggling, you know. He could be my little brother."

Clay wants a brother? My stomach cinches up again and I have to lean against my bedroom wall to steady myself. What about me?

Somehow they get on the topic of the bag Anton told Nana he saw Clay carrying this morning. I guess Clay's tired of lying, and like I said, he's not very good at it, so he admits he spends his Mondays collecting donations of clothing and toiletries for the homeless support group.

Granddad reminds Clay that he didn't sign the permission slip the homeless help network needs before kids can volunteer. Clay calmly tells him that wasn't necessary because he used Nana's name. Yes, you heard that right. He forged Nana's name on the permission slip. Something that is definitely wrong.

That's when things go ballistic. *B-A-L-L-I-S-T-I-C.*

Go ballistic: to fly into a rage

Clay's bedroom door is slammed shut and the ceiling above my head starts to shake. Please believe me when I say I'm surprised our house still has a roof. Granddad trumpets like a herd of mad elephants while Nana tells Clay off in a mean whisper buzz. I have to tiptoe halfway up the stairs to hear her. She sounds like a really mad hive of bees.

"BZZZZZ . . . I trusted you . . . BZZZZZ . . . How dare you . . . BZZZZZ . . . I never thought you'd . . ."

We've never had this much drama in our house and it scares me. I'm sitting on the stairs with my right hand in my mouth without even realizing it. I mean, I haven't bitten my nails since I was seven or eight years old.

Our neighbor Mr. Charles comes over to make sure we're all right. I'm the one who goes down to answer the door.

"Y'all don't usually make such a racket," he says, peering over my shoulder. "I could barely hear the eleven o'clock news." Mr. Charles adds that he was already upset after he heard how the city hall rally almost turned violent. "Reminds me of my time in the National Guard," he says.

Is that why Clay looked so scared when he got home? And Mama and Daddy are halfway around the world partying? I look over at their wedding photo on the mantel and I just want to turn it around. They have to come home.

Mr. Charles leaves and I put my hands over my ears to

try to block out the chaos coming from the third floor of our house. I go through the kitchen and take the back staircase up to my room and calculate the time. It's eleven fifteen at night here, five fifteen in the morning in Amsterdam. Mama and Daddy are probably not up yet but if I had a phone I would call them. I don't so I sit down at my desk and write a stupid slow email.

Subject: Turmoil (a state of great disturbance, confusion, or uncertainty)

Your tour may be going great but things here at home are not. Everybody's mad at everybody else and there's a lot of shouting. It got so bad that Mr. Charles had to come over and check on us. Can you please come home? Please?

Chapter Fifteen

CONCEALMENT

n. l. the action of hiding something or preventing it from being known: *The concealment of the body.* *2.* something that acts as a hiding place or cover

I hear every little creak and groan our old house makes through the whole night. It's like the house has to pull itself back together after so much fighting. I wake up confused and reach over to where my phone should be on my bedside table, but it's not there. There's nothing there so I just lie in my twisted-up sheets and turn everything that's happened over and over in my mind. What did Clay say about Anton's family? We're struggling too.

I drag myself up and get dressed, grabbing my light gray sweatshirt and pulling it on over my yellow tee before going downstairs. I stick my head out the front door to see if Jamila's on our porch but she's not there. Is she sick? That's the only reason why she ever misses a day.

"Neva, come and get your breakfast," Nana calls.

I'm hungry but breakfast doesn't go down easy. Granddad sits at the table reading his *Philadelphia Inquirer* without talking to anybody. Clay inhales his oatmeal as quickly as he can so he can escape to the swim club. He's lucky Nana didn't totally ground him. Mrs. Giles needs him and my grandmother loves her some Mrs. Giles. So Clay's only allowed out of the house to go to the swim club to work, not to hang with his friends. Nana says there will be major trouble if Clay goes anywhere else. Yeah, she sounds like Granddad now.

Nana has dark circles under her eyes and moves slower than usual. Drama isn't her thing. She'd much rather be having fun with me and Clay instead of punishing somebody. I look around our pretty dining room. It still looks nice but it has a bad feeling to it now. Negative energy. That's what it is. It never felt like this when Mama and Daddy were home.

Clay gets up to leave and Granddad says, "That rally you went to yesterday didn't end so well." He puts his paper down. "Better be careful."

Clay rolls his eyes but keeps his mouth shut. He grabs

his backpack and makes a big show of heaving it onto his shoulders and adjusting the straps.

Poor Clay. There's a reason why he's Mrs. Giles's best lifeguard. I can't think of anybody else who cares about people as much as he does.

I'm not sure if Clay wants my company, especially since I heard him wishing for a brother last night, but I gobble down the last of my toast and ask if I can walk with him at least as far as Jamila's street.

"Be back in half an hour. We have to get you a new phone," Nana says before adding, "Clay, is yours charged? I don't want any nonsense today."

My grandparents say they miss the peacefulness of the times when everybody didn't have a cell, but they can't live without them now just like everybody else.

Me and Clay step out into the sunshine and I have to practically run to keep up with him. "Something's going on with them." He says it like none of this is his fault.

"Yeah, they're really mad at you."

Clay sucks his teeth but a flicker of shame crosses his face. "I shouldn't have forged Nana's name. I know that. But what I don't understand is why they aren't more upset about everything that's happening out here. Why aren't they more political?"

Clay uses that word that seems to be everywhere these days.

Political: relating to the government or the public affairs of a country; relating to the ideas or strategies of a particular party or group in a society

Is my brother referring to what's happening politically in the country or politically inside our house? Our grandparents are definitely upset about what's happening with us. If Clay was running for office in our family right now the only vote he'd get would be mine.

"Mama and Dad are part of the problem too," he says.

"Is that what Daddy talks to you about in his cards? He only writes me about music and how the tour is going."

Clay nods. "Sometimes I think Mama and Dad are more traditional than Nana and Granddad. They were active back in the day, you know."

"Granddad and Nana?"

Clay nods again. "They did their part. That's why I thought everything would be cool this summer. But I see now there's no reasoning with Granddad. Going undercover is the only way to deal with him."

"Tell me about it." Clay looks down at me but he doesn't ask for any details. "Maybe Mama and Daddy will come home early," I add.

Clay snorts. "Don't count on it."

My stomach does a little backflip but I try not to show it.

"Why are you wearing that sweatshirt?" Clay asks. "Aren't you hot?"

I look down my front. My breasts aren't so obvious under my sweatshirt, but I'm sure not going to discuss that with my brother.

"Try to stay out of trouble today, okay?" That's what comes out of my mouth.

"And you stay beautiful," he answers.

Chapter Sixteen

JEALOUS

adj. 1. feeling or showing envy of someone or their achievements and advantages *2.* feeling or showing suspicion of someone's unfaithfulness in a relationship: *A jealous friend.*

It's hot. Ninety degrees and sunny. This sweatshirt is killing me but I run down Jamila's street like I'm in the Penn Relays. She may be sick or something. Why else didn't she come over this morning? I'm sorting through everything in my head but it's hard to decide where to start. I'll tell her about me and Clay first, then Clay and Nana, and then everything else.

But when I get to Jamila's front door I hear dance music, highlife. It's what her daddy plays when he's in a good mood. Jamila can't be sick.

Their front door pops open and Jamila bursts out. "Guess what?" she says. "We're going away on vacation."

"Va . . . ca . . . tion," I stammer. "When?"

"We're going to Ghana in two weeks."

Jamila's daddy joins us out on the porch and twirls her around. "Neva, we are so happy," he says. "I'm finally going to take my family to visit home."

Jamila looks up at him and a big grin breaks out across her face. She's smiling like Mrs. Giles over at the swim club. Her daddy reaches down and tickles her under her arm and Jamila doubles over laughing.

Jamila's baby brother starts to cry inside the house and Mr. Mensah leans toward the door and cups his ear. "Neva," he says, "my son has a very strong voice. Eh?"

"So, you're not sick?" That's the wrong answer but I don't know what else to say.

Mr. Mensah frowns. "No one is sick in this house, ooh. We're celebrating." He looks at my sweatshirt. "You have to be careful in this heat. Jamila, go and fetch your friend a glass of water."

Jamila scurries inside and Mr. Mensah pulls one of the white plastic chairs over for me to sit on. "And how are your parents, the famous musicians?"

I know he's trying to make me feel good but asking

about Mama and Daddy only makes me hotter than I already am.

"I don't know," I say. "I haven't spoken to them today."

"Eh?" He frowns again. "I imagine they have a very busy schedule. Plus, there's the time difference. I know it can be difficult to reach people back home because of that."

Jamila comes out with a big glass of water with ice cubes, lemon, and mint in it. "Straight from your garden," she says. Her eyes are sparkling like she's never seen water before. Pure joy.

Joy: a feeling of great pleasure and happiness

That's what's on her face. But I'm not a part of it.

Mr. Mensah sits back for a few minutes nodding his head in time to the music. He closes his eyes and starts moving his shoulders like he's the happiest man in the world. He doesn't stop until the song ends.

"Time to get over to the shop," he says, checking his watch. "Eh, Jamila, don't let your friend get too much sun, ooh." He touches my arm lightly before getting up and giving Jamila a hug.

I gulp down the whole glass of ice water with my eyes closed. I wipe my mouth with the back of my hand and try to focus on the horns and guitars in the new song that's surrounding me. The beat usually makes me move but not now. I'm sitting stock-still.

Mr. Mensah's gone when I reopen my eyes.

"I tried to call you last night to tell you about the trip," says Jamila. "There's nothing wrong between my parents. My *paapa*'s just been working extra jobs to get the money together."

That's her explanation for not coming over to our house this morning? Doesn't she care that I was afraid she was in the hospital? I thought she got hit by a car or something. Everything may be great at her house but mine is crumbling.

That big hole that I'm afraid of falling down into is right here on Jamila's porch. It's stretching wider and wider until it's too big for me to jump over. I'm looking at her real close to see if she senses it too. I need to know but I'm afraid to ask.

"My phone died." That's what comes out. "Nana's taking me—"

"What about the bra-thing?" she interrupts. "How did Clay act when he saw you?"

The bra-thing? That's how she describes what happened to me yesterday? The worst day of my life?

I'm sitting here on my best friend's porch listening to music I can't feel when it hits me. She doesn't care.

I tilt my water glass so the few remaining ice cubes swirl around the bottom. "Clay was cool," I say. "He didn't try to make me feel bad . . . although he could have."

I'm talking about Clay being cool but I'm blazing hot even though I just drank a whole glass of water.

"See," she says. "I knew you were making a big deal out of nothing."

A big deal out of nothing? I stand up and hand the now-empty glass back to Jamila. Our fingers touch on the cold glass but I don't look up at her.

"Aren't you hot in that—" she begins.

"I gotta go," I say. "Nana's waiting for me."

I jump down off her porch and make it back home in half the time it took me to get there.

Chapter Seventeen

BONDING

n. l. a relationship that usually begins at the time of birth between family members and that establishes the basis for an ongoing mutual attachment: *The siblings' bonding started the moment they laid eyes on each other.* *2.* a close friendship that develops between people often as the result of shared intense experiences, as those shared in military combat

Me and Nana take the trolley down to Nineteenth Street. This is Center City and it's totally different from West Philly. For one thing, I don't see any signs for activist jobs taped to light poles. I don't see any of the Little Free Library wooden book boxes either, but there are a lot of tall buildings that block out most of the sun. They tower over the statute of William Penn, the Englishman who named the state after his father, on the top of city hall.

"I remember when buildings weren't allowed to be taller than Billy Penn's hat," says Nana, shaking her head. "Now, well, just look around."

She's walking slow, but as usual, what I'm wearing doesn't escape her inspection.

"I'm surprised you're wearing that sweatshirt," she says. "Aren't you hot?"

"Jamila's whole family is going to Ghana," I say, ignoring her question. "Not just her parents, her whole family." My voice quivers a little on the word *family* and Nana's quick glance over at me tells me she heard it.

Nana asks me to remind her to call Jamila's mama tonight. "I know they've been wanting to make that trip for a long time," she says.

I've noticed she and Granddad always prefer to call somebody from home. It's like they think random folks on the street want to hear what they're saying. Must be an old people thing.

"You could call her right now," I say, lashing out even though I know that's not fair.

Nana looks at me again but she lets my smart remark slide. Instead she does something so tender that it breaks through the wall I've built around myself. She leans over and says as softly as she can, "You don't have to hide yourself under a sweatshirt, Neva. I tried that when I was your age and it didn't make any difference."

I don't look at her but the truth is I'm burning up in this thing and mad at myself for even putting it on.

We get my new phone and sit in Dilworth Park right outside city hall. Nana buys me a cherry water ice and gets a cappuccino for herself. "I don't normally spend my money on this expensive stuff," she says, "but if I don't take care of myself nobody else will."

Nana's statement pulls me out of the reruns of Jamila's betrayal I've been playing in my head. My grandmother's making a point about something but I'm not exactly sure what it is since we haven't seen any half-naked women ads or girls wearing shoes they can't walk in. That's another one of the things she hates. Stilettoes. *Don't buy shoes you can't walk in, Neva.* How many times have I heard that?

We walk over to a little blue table with yellow and green chairs and I pull the gray sweatshirt off over my head. Nana smiles and smooths down the back of my T-shirt as we sit.

She picks up a flyer left behind by somebody else. MARCH FOR JUSTICE is splashed across the top in big letters. There's a lot more little writing on the flyer but I can't make it out because I'm sitting across from her and trying to read upside down. It's set for this coming Sunday, June 24.

Nana reads the flyer and sighs. I can't tell if she's for or against the march, so I ask, "Are you going to march? Clay told me you and Granddad used to do stuff like that."

"Yes, we did." She says it like it's a fact I should have known, but we've never talked about this before. "But I thought the need for that was over."

"Have you ever been arrested?"

"Me . . . no," she says. "But that doesn't mean I haven't stood up against things that weren't right." She sighs. "I had hoped for much better for you. That's all."

She doesn't elaborate and I don't press her because my water ice is melting faster than I can eat it. I lean forward so it'll drip on the ground and not on my yellow top, so I don't see Anton walking over to us.

"Hi, Miss Cecily." Anton stands next to our little table. He nods at me but he's standing real stiff like he doesn't know what to do. "How's Clay?" he asks, looking down at the flyer on our table. His head is tilted and I can see his long, dark eyelashes.

"Clay's grounded," Nana says. "So you're not going to see much of him for a while."

Anton looks up and his hazel eyes widen. "Oh, okay," he says. "So . . . I . . . I guess he won't be at the march."

Nana shakes her head no.

Nana's not mean but she shouldn't have said that. Not only is Clay grounded but now Nana's told one of his boys about it. It's always better if you break that sort of news to your friends yourself. It's no telling how the story will get twisted once Anton puts the word out.

Anton backs up and says he guesses he'll see us at the swim club. He smiles at me before he disappears down into the subway entrance.

"That boy likes you," Nana says, folding up the flyer and putting it in her purse. "You all are too young for that."

Nana's mistaken. Anton likes Michelle Overton, but I'm not about to bring her name up again. Not if I can help it. I study my grandmother and she looks, what's the word? *Resolute?*

Resolute: admirably purposeful, determined, and unwavering

Yeah, she's real resolute.

The softness she had in her voice when she convinced me to take off my sweatshirt is all gone. Her jaw is set real tight and the last thing I want to do is set her off on one of her lectures about boys.

"Clay really wants to go on Sunday," I say, bringing the subject back to the march. "Can't you lift his grounding for just one day?"

Nana fastens her eyes on mine. "Clay totally disrespected me," she says. She waits, like, a full minute so what she just said sinks in. "Did you notice he didn't try forging Granddad's name? Who does he think I am, Mayor Chump?"

Now, this is another one of the things I've noticed about old people. They come up with these names nobody's ever heard of. Mayor Chump? Did she say that because we're sitting here in front of city hall? I have no idea, but the hurt in her eyes tells me she's just told me something she'd probably never say to anybody else.

Chapter Eighteen

(A) REVELATION

n. 1. a surprising and previously unknown fact, especially one that is made known in a dramatic way: *Revelations about his personal life.* *2.* a remarkable quality of someone or something: *Seeing them play at the international level was a revelation.*

Clay's home right on time so there's no trouble. He usually comes in the back door, stops in the kitchen, grabs something to eat like a box of graham crackers or a whole pack of Fig Newtons, and washes it down with half a carton of milk, which he drinks straight out of the carton. You know what that means.

Backwash: the liquid that flows back into a bottle, glass, etc. after someone has taken a drink, assumed to contain that person's saliva

I hate it.

But a spooky silence has settled over our house. Clay comes in the front door to avoid Nana in the kitchen and goes straight up to his room. He doesn't come back down until I go up to tell him it's time to eat.

"I'm not hungry," he says.

I'm leaning against the upstairs banister and that lump in my throat that I have so much trouble pushing down tries to rise up again. But of course he can't see it. He's all tied up with his own problems. I wasn't making it up when I told Mama I was all alone.

"You are too hungry." That's what comes out.

Clay opens his mouth to come back at me but I cut him off by telling him about Jamila's family trip.

"Wow," he says. "A lot of folks traveling this summer, huh?" He doesn't say more than that but his pursed lips tell me he's just as jealous as I am.

"Did Anton tell you about the march?" I ask.

"Yeah," he says, "but I already knew about it."

I wait to see if Clay's pissed off 'cause Nana put the word out about his grounding, but I don't think he knows she did that. So, Anton didn't tell anybody? Does that mean Anton doesn't have any friends or is he just cool like that?

"Michelle told me about it," he says.

My fingers go to the shoulders of my yellow top and I

adjust my bra straps although they don't really need it. Michelle. She's a trigger that makes people in my family lose all sense.

"Food's getting cold," Granddad yells up two flights of stairs. "Next thing I know you'll be telling folks I don't feed you right."

Clay looks at me and shakes his head. "Granddad needs a cause. Holding those babies over at the hospital isn't enough."

"What?"

"You don't know about his volunteering?"

"'Course I do."

"But you don't know what he actually does." Clay lets me hang for a few seconds before going on. "Granddad and Mr. Charles hold babies that don't have parents to take care of them. You know, babies that have been abandoned and whatnot."

Whatnot has a bad sound to it. I don't want to think about what else goes along with abandonment.

What babies need is love, but the idea of Granddad and Mr. Charles taking care of newborns, that's wild. You have to be quiet around babies. No acting out or saying weird stuff. I can't imagine Granddad being mellow unless, maybe, he has another side? Another side that's hard to see especially at times like now.

"I'm not going to ask y'all to come down here again . . ." he bellows.

Bellow: to emit a deep, loud roar, typically in pain or anger

Trust me, that's the only word to describe his yelling.

"Come on," says Clay, leaving his room and walking over to the top of the stairs. "I do not want a repeat of last night."

Chapter Nineteen

DRAFTED

v. 1. prepared a preliminary version of (a text): *He drafted a letter of resignation.* *2.* selected (a person or group of people) for a certain purpose such as military service or a sports team: *She was drafted to help with the new task force.*

Dinner is pretty much like breakfast. Not Nana's crab cakes, but the mood. Nana keeps asking—no, telling—Clay to do lots of stuff she usually does herself or gets me to do. Like, *Go get more rolls* or *Take the ice cream out of the freezer.* And she doesn't even say please. Now, I'm not saying he shouldn't help out more around the house, but it's just funny how she's heaping every single thing on him.

Granddad looks at Nana every time she gives Clay an order but he doesn't say anything. And I'm looking at Granddad trying to picture a baby in his arms. Not an easy thing to do although he must have done it when my mama was born.

I get up to clear the table but Nana stops me. "It's Clay's turn," she says.

Granddad's eyes widen but he's smart enough to keep quiet. What he does is he gets up and starts helping Clay.

"Fine," says Nana. "Neva and I can relax for a change."

I fix my eyes on the light blue embroidered place mat that's sitting in front of me. Its little red flowers are pretty, but what's going on here is the exact opposite. Nana is making a point. Constantly. She's putting Clay in his place big-time. And nobody's challenging her either.

I think about what Nana said to me before. You know, when I asked if Clay could go to the march. *Clay totally disrespected me.* She is not having that.

I don't know how far this is all going to go but our beautiful dining room feels like a battlefield and I've been pulled to her side. I sit there fingering the place mat for a little longer because I don't want to leave her alone, but it's weird because we're not talking or anything.

Granddad and Clay stay in the kitchen after they clear the table, but I can hear them arguing about how to stack the dishwasher. Nana still hasn't said anything to me so I just sit there frozen until I get up the nerve to excuse myself from the table.

Up in my room, I pick up the mystery series I started last week, but I have to read each sentence three times over to understand anything. That's not really reading. I don't know what to even call it so I close my book and go back to rerunning everything that's happened over and over in my head. Ruminating. That's what it's called when you think very, very deeply about something.

I reach for my dictionary and run my fingers down its worn spine. It's a little wobbly in places but it's still strong enough to hold all the pages together.

My phone rings and I grab it.

"Hey, girl," says Michelle. She sounds real friendly like we've known each other for a million years. "I'm so tired. I just spent the whole day at the community center with my dad and some teachers talking about ways to disrupt the school-to-prison pipeline."

She says it like I should know what she's talking about. I don't respond and she calls me on it.

"You know what that is, right?"

"No . . . not really."

"Okay, quick definition." She pauses for a few seconds and I try to look it up real fast while she's thinking. "It refers to how kids get suspended or expelled from school unnecessarily and then end up in the criminal justice system. You know, jail."

"Oh," I say. "I don't really know about that."

"Yes, you do," she says. "Just think about Anton's brother. You know about this."

"I do?" I say slowly.

There's a silence that tells me I've said the wrong thing again.

"You should ask your brother about that sometime," she says.

What does that mean? Why can't she tell me herself?

Michelle goes on. "I was just calling to see if you want to hang out tomorrow morning," she says. "I need a break from all of this."

I'm not really sure what all *this* is but I don't say no to hanging out with her again. She was cool at the swim club, and besides, Jamila's going away on her trip so she's not going to be spending every morning with me anymore. Might as well get used to that now.

That's what I tell myself but it feels like the strands of my friendship with Jamila are coming loose. Like our friendship, another thing that's been important to me for so long, is no longer there. Me and Jamila on our porch every morning. Is that just going to slip away like the peace in our house? I don't want it to, but how come I feel hot every time I think about how quickly Jamila dismissed me? The bra-thing. How could she say that?

"Let's meet at the library," I say before hanging up with Michelle. I may be confused about everything she's talking about, but I'm not simple enough to open up the Michelle Overton box with my grandparents by having her come over here in the morning.

I go back to looking up the school-to-prison pipeline and see there's more to it than what Michelle said. A lot more. It sounds like it's really hard for kids who've been in jail to get back into a good situation in school. Is that why Anton tries so hard to send books to his brother? I don't know, but there's running on the stairs so I open my door, hoping to flag Clay down to ask him about it.

What? He totally plays me off like I'm not even standing here. Now he's really got an attitude. He can't be afraid I'm going to tease him about cleaning up the kitchen or something dumb like that. I want to ask him about how kids end up in jail, but he doesn't even look at me.

I hear Granddad and Nana downstairs arguing. Something about doing the right thing and they don't want Mama and Daddy mad at them.

I sit down in the hallway and rest my head on my bent knees. The only thing I see is my stomach rising and falling every time I take a breath, and that reminds me of Mama's advice. What does she always say? Try to breathe deeply especially when you sing. I take a few more slow, deep breaths to calm myself down.

"Clay-ay," I call up to his room in a friendly voice. I helped him out with Nana and Granddad yesterday. That has to count for something.

Clay doesn't answer but the music coming out of his room gets louder. He's mad because he had to do the dishes? I help Nana clean up the kitchen all the time. I don't really like it but I don't complain about it.

I go back into my room and look across the street to Michelle Overton's house. She's probably sitting on the couch with her daddy right now. I'll bet they're not arguing either. They're probably talking about their meetings with teachers and all that other stuff. I'll ask her to explain it again tomorrow since my brother's not talking to me tonight.

I sit down at my desk and text Jamila that I'll be busy in the morning. I'm not the one cutting the cord. She's done that already.

Chapter Twenty

INTIMIDATION

n. the action of intimidating someone or the state of being made timid or filled with fear through the force of personality or by superior display of wealth, talent, beauty, etc: *Ineffective teachers sometimes rely on intimidation to keep the students quiet.*

The *library.* That word has a special ring for everybody in my family. I like the library because it has a limitless supply of books. And Granddad and Nana, well, they're so proud of how much I like to read that they never question going to the library. I could probably ask to go there at twelve midnight or six in the morning and they'd say yes. So it's no problem to tell them I have to return a book today or it'll be late.

How do you spell late fees? A-L-L-O-W-A-N-C-E. I don't have to tell you who said that. Granddad's in a foul mood this morning so he doesn't press me about Jamila not being here.

"She's getting ready for her trip," I say, and that's that.

I walk Spruce Street's long, hot blocks down past the Penn Alexander School to the library, hoping nobody bothers me. I never used to worry about being harassed, but now I worry about running into those loud guys again. Is this what it's going to be like from now on? I miss the days of just being silly and loose and free when I'm outside.

I cut over to Locust when I get to Forty-Second Street because I like the redbrick sidewalks. They're pretty and they go with the old stone houses. I've seen girls having a hard time walking this stretch of sidewalk in high heels, though. They have to go real slow and keep looking down to avoid getting their heels caught in the cracks. Spoils their look if you ask me.

I get to the library but I don't see Michelle on the ground floor so I go upstairs to the big room with the tall beamed ceiling. Every computer is taken, as usual, but I see Michelle sitting at one of them. I walk over and there's Anton sitting at the next little computer cubicle.

"Hey," Michelle says. "Look who I ran into."

So, she didn't invite him? He just happened to be here? I feel my face getting warm but that's stupid, right? I mean this is the public library. Public means it's open to everybody.

"Hey," says Anton. "We were just reading about DOC's reversing their book ban."

He smiles at me but I look straight at the computer screen. What's DOC? Already I feel out of my league.

"You have to break it down for her," says Michelle. "She's not up on how this state treats incarcerated folk."

"I know what's going on," I say, looking directly at her. "Anton collects books to send to people in jail."

"Yeah," he says. "That was before the Department of Corrections changed their mail and visitation policies."

"Why would they—"

"Excuse me," says the librarian, putting her right index finger to her lips. "You're going to have to continue your conversation outside."

"Sorry," says Anton. "I was just leaving." He logs out of the computer and whispers under his breath, "I know you just got here but are you staying inside?"

I shake my head no, ignoring Michelle's stare.

We get outside and Anton starts talking again before the doors have even fully closed. He doesn't wait for us to decide where to go or anything.

"See, Neva, folks used to be able to mail books to people in prison, but then the DOC, Department of

Corrections, changed their policy so folks caught up in the system could only buy preapproved books from the prison system itself."

I knew that part from the poster I saw in Clay's closet but I didn't know the law was different now.

"But now there's a change?" I ask.

Anton nods. "Big-time reversal. The community protested and got the state to reverse their policy so I can send books to my brother again."

Anton's voice goes down when he mentions his brother and I see a darkness in his light eyes. It must be a hard thing to talk about.

"I'm sorry about your brother," I say, "but the law switching back is good news. Right?"

"It is," says Anton, "but some of DOC's other policies are wrong—"

"You guys," Michelle says. "I asked Neva to hang because I needed a break, okay? I thought we'd check out some clothes or do something else like that."

Anton frowns and his eyes narrow for a second. "You got me," he finally says, throwing up his hands. "Once I get started on this stuff there's no stopping me. But I'm not into clothes so . . . I'm out."

He smiles when he says *I'm out* so I know he's not mad.

"See you at tomorrow's meeting," Michelle says as Anton takes a swig from his water bottle and walks toward Walnut Street.

Michelle sighs. "Clay'll be there tomorrow, right?"

"Be where?" I ask.

Michelle looks at me hard.

"Didn't Clay tell you?"

"Tell me what?"

"About the march. The March for Justice."

"Oh, yeah. Clay knows about it."

"Knows about it?" Michelle's voice rises. "He's one of the youth organizers."

So, okay, Clay hasn't told Michelle that he can't go. She doesn't know he's grounded and I definitely don't think I'm the one to tell her.

"Well," she says, "I've been calling him but he's not answering. Tell him there's another planning meeting tomorrow. He needs to be there and you . . . you should think about coming too. We need all the help we can get."

Me? I never said I wanted to be a part of this.

"I . . . I have to . . . I have to ask my grandparents," I stammer, "about the meeting, I mean."

"Oh," says Michelle. "That means no."

All the friendliness goes out of her voice. It's like a big

gust of wind came down the street and blew all the good feelings between us away. I don't know what to say. She said she needed a break so why the attitude?

I suggest hanging out on Locust Walk, but she shakes her head no. We stand outside the library for a few more awkward minutes but it's no good. She's talking about all this stuff that I don't know anything about.

"You heard what Anton said," she says, turning toward the nail salon across the street. "Now is not the time for lightweights."

That's not what Anton said at all, but I don't challenge Michelle. Why do I let her get away with that? I thought she didn't want to talk about that kind of stuff today. I know my own mind and I know I've got something great going on deep inside me. So why can't I bring it up to the light? It's like my brain is hiding behind dark clouds, like the ones gathering overhead.

I trudge back into the library and climb the stairs up to the children's department. The librarian looks up and smiles, but I don't smile back. My problem is I'm too proud to call Jamila and too intimidated by Michelle to call her out so I sit here all by myself. I told Mama I was all alone. Why wouldn't she believe me?

It's raining hard by the time I leave the library and

that's just fine. No one can see my long face under my umbrella.

I slip into our house and go straight to my room. I call Mama's number but I only get her message with one of her songs playing in the background. Her voice usually soothes me but now it only churns up more bad feelings.

Chapter Twenty-one

POSTURING

n. behaving in a way that is intended to impress or mislead others: *A masking of fear with macho posturing.*

Nana and Granddad are not night owls but they usually stay up until after the eleven o'clock news. Another old people's favorite thing. Mr. Charles watches it too. But not tonight. Tonight my grandparents go to bed early.

There's soft music coming from Clay's room so I go up and knock on his door. I miss the talks we used to have and I hope he misses me a little bit too.

Clay doesn't answer right away so I knock again. He must have been out on his balcony because I hear the screen door open and close.

"Just a minute," he says. His lips are pulled tight when he opens the door.

"What's up?" he says.

"That's what I came to ask you."

Clay's shoulders slump. "I thought you went to bed."

"Very funny, Clay. I don't sleep with Granddad and Nana."

"Well . . . what's on your mind?"

"I just wanted to talk to you."

"Can't it wait until tomorrow?"

"No. You blew past me yesterday like I didn't even exist and I haven't seen you all day today." I say that last part even though I've been hiding out in my room since I came back from the library.

There's a scraping sound on Clay's balcony like somebody's moving one of the chairs around.

"You have company?"

"Can't I do anything in this house without being watched?"

"I'm not watching you, but who's out there?"

"Neva," Clay sighs. "You're twelve and I'm sixteen. Has it ever occurred to you that I might have stuff to do that doesn't involve you?"

"But it involves Michelle?" I blurt that out without thinking. Something that seems to be happening more and more these past few days. I used to be more careful with my words. "Is she up here?"

Clay frowns and lowers his voice. "No. She is not. But what if she was? She's older than you," he says. "And . . . and more aware." He averts his eyes so he's not looking right at me.

Nana's meatballs are turning over in my stomach, and even though it's hard to do, I keep my eyes directly on Clay. So, he thinks I'm not aware. What am I? Just the cute little sister? The other day he said I was really something but it looks like that something isn't very much. I'm starting to shake so I plant my feet far apart like he does when he needs to look big.

"I know about the march, Clay, and I'm going to the meeting tomorrow."

I don't know where that came from, but there, I said it.

The balcony door opens and Anton steps into Clay's room. Clay jerks his head back to look at him.

"I should go," says Anton, pulling at his right ear. "We were just talking about the march but I don't want to cause any trouble." He avoids looking directly at me but I can hear the concern in his voice.

"Don't worry about it, man. Everything's cool."

So, Clay has time to hang with Anton but he doesn't have time for me? He really does wish he had a brother instead of . . .

"You don't have to go anywhere," Clay says to Anton.

My neck starts stiffening up and I don't know what to say so I repeat myself.

"I'm going to the meeting tomorrow."

"Good luck with that," says Clay, turning back to me. "You know they won't let you." He doesn't have to say who *they* are. "Have you even asked them?"

I don't answer right away. I know my grandparents will say no if I ask so . . . maybe . . . I don't ask. Nana's not the only person who's been disrespected. I shrug my shoulders and hope I look cool but my stomach's churning again. I've put my foot into something that I don't know how to get out of, but I can't back down. For some reason, I can't lose face on this.

Chapter Twenty-Two

MISERY

n. a state or feeling of great distress or discomfort of mind or body: *She went upstairs and cried in misery.*

There's an email from Daddy when I wake up in the morning.

> Your grandparents are very upset. What is going on? Will skype with you and Clay at eight a.m.

Clay knocks on my door, sputtering, which is totally not like him. "I got this, Neva. Let me take the lead when we talk to Dad."

"He probably knows everything, Clay. He spoke to Nana and Granddad already."

My brother collapses against the open door frame. "I may never get off punishment now."

Is that all he's worried about? He's not upset about all

the drama that's going on in our house? He has no idea of how much he hurt Nana or how he made me feel last night?

Clay looks at me and points up to the ceiling. "Let's do what we gotta do upstairs," he says. "More privacy."

We get up to Clay's room a few minutes before Daddy calls and Clay's pacing makes me nervous. He's normally Mr. Cool but he must be afraid I'm going to tell on him.

"I won't say anything about Anton," I say, "but you should know I asked Mama and Daddy to come home."

"Great," Clay says, shrugging as he turns on his laptop.

We didn't plan to but we end up sitting together on Clay's desk chair and Daddy's tired face fills the screen. The bags under his eyes look like suitcases and his nose is huge. He's not hung up on proper lighting or anything like that.

"All right, you two. What exactly is going on?"

Clay goes into a long story about how Granddad and Nana are out of step with what's happening in the world and are stopping him from supporting his friend Anton. I see what he's doing. Blaming our grandparents instead of taking it right to Mama and Daddy, even though they're the ones who told him to chill this summer. Playing politics? Is that what Clay's doing?

"So you forged your grandmother's signature to do something you know could be dangerous," Daddy says.

"It's not dangerous, Dad. Everybody's doing it."

"I don't care what everybody's doing, man. How many times do we have to go over this? Your mama and I do not want you out in the streets while we're away."

Clay hangs his head. "I admitted I was wrong. But Nana just won't let it go and now she's all over me."

"Clay, there's no excuse for what you did. None."

Clay slumps forward on our chair so Daddy can't see his face anymore.

"Where's Mama?" I ask. "Did she get my message?"

"Yes." Daddy sighs. "She has your messages. All of them." He scratches his head before continuing. "You know, Neva, this isn't easy. We were out very late last night with all the extra shows."

"Extra shows?"

"Yes. Your mama is really on fire on this tour. Everybody loves her." Daddy pauses and smiles a little bit. "To be honest, I'm just hanging on to her coattails. Your mama is fabulous! She's trying to get some rest now but . . . she doesn't need all these distractions. You hear what I'm saying? It's tearing her up inside."

Mama's upset about not being here? I thought she was happy being on the scene, hanging out at parties and speaking a new language.

"So, is she coming home?"

"Not yet. This tour is very important for us. It may be our, or her . . . It may be her last chance to put herself out there. So, guys, she needs your support."

Clay sits back up.

"Do you hear me?" Daddy asks. "Clay, no more drama?"

"It's not drama it's—"

"Did you hear what I said?"

Clay sighs but nods his head.

"Neva?" Daddy says. "No more disturbing messages?"

I can't answer because my heart is sinking. Disturbing messages? How can he say that? Mama said she'd come home if things didn't work out and they're not. They're not working out at all. I turn my head away from the screen because I feel my face collapsing into itself.

"Neva?" Daddy says again.

Daddy can't see me as I slide down in the chair but words I can't control slip out of my mouth. "Who does she think she is?"

I wish I hadn't said that, but my chin is trembling and the rest of my face is resting against the back of my brother's shirt.

Clay turns around and tries to hug me but I push his arms away.

"Neva," I hear Daddy saying. "We can't leave the tour.

Do you know how much trouble that would cause Ms. G? We signed a contract. I'm sorry, but it just can't happen right now."

I slide down to the floor with only a whimper on my lips.

Chapter Twenty-Three

STALEMATE

n. 1. a situation in which further action or progress by opposing or competing parties seems impossible: *The war had again reached a stalemate.* *2.* (chess) a position counting as a draw, in which a player is not in check but cannot move except into check

Granddad and Nana fuss over me instead of arguing with each other. Granddad pats my shoulder after we eat and tells me not to worry about cleaning up.

I stick my head out the front door mainly because that's what I always do. I'm not expecting Jamila, but here she is at our little front gate. She's here even though I blew her off yesterday. She stands like she doesn't know what to do for a minute, pulling at her red polka-dot shorts that are the same shade of red as her bike, before leaning her bike up against our little garden fence and walking up to the porch.

"You have no idea what's been going on," I say, pulling her arm. I'm gushing because it seems like ages since we've been together on our porch. Our porch. Where we confide in each other and work everything out.

"I've been busy too," she says. "We're getting ready for our trip."

Granddad hasn't gone to volunteer over at the hospital this morning. He and Nana are in the living room talking about whether they should plant more bulbs in our backyard in the fall. Very sweet.

Me and Jamila move down to the garden so we're out of earshot and I start telling her about how Ms. G's whole tour would be ruined if Mama left, and Clay being grounded, and Nana's taking him down on everything he does, and Michelle wanting me to go to the planning meeting for the march. But I don't tell her the part about Michelle leaving me at the library. That part I leave out.

"You and Michelle?" Jamila says. "Going to what meeting?"

I bring her up-to-date on Michelle talking to me at the pool and the two of us walking home together and her asking me to be a part of her work. Jamila frowns a little when I tell her about the guys harassing us on the street. "That happens to my mama a lot," she says. "It doesn't matter what you have on."

I go back to telling her how I asked my mama to come home but then my daddy talked with me and Clay this morning and told us our mama is a star. A star. I should be happy about that and part of me is but another part, a bigger part, wants her back home.

"Maybe she'll make it to Ghana," Jamila says. "Wouldn't it be cool if I saw your mama singing in Accra?"

Is she listening to me at all? Everything's about her trip.

"My auntie knows a lot of people in Ghana. I bet she could get your mama and *paapa* some gigs there," she continues.

Gigs in Ghana? That's the last thing I want. Jamila rattles on about how much fun it's going to be to fly, and how her auntie's going to show her everything—Elmina Castle and Independence Arch. Whatever that is.

She really doesn't know how I feel? She's just like everybody else. She's rattling on about her trip, but I just cut her off.

"I'm going to be hanging out with Michelle this afternoon," I say. "I'm going to take up the slack now that Clay's grounded."

Jamila hugs her knees to her chest. "I didn't know you were so political," she says.

"We all need to be more enlightened," I say. "You know, we should all be bringing something to the table."

Jamila's eyes narrow but she doesn't have a response to that. She picks up a handful of dirt and lets it run through her fingers. "Are you doing all this because of Michelle?"

"Not because of Michelle," I say. "I'm doing it because it's the right thing to do." I say it like I'm being interviewed on National Public Radio, but I don't look at her because then she'll know something outside of me is pushing me to talk like this. She'll see how Clay hurt my feelings when he said I'm not sophisticated or, what word did he use, *aware*. And if she looks deep enough, she'll see how jealous I am of her. She gets to smell her mama's lavender-scented fingers every single day and dance with her daddy. They'll all be together in West Africa. She'll probably come home wearing beautiful head wraps. Wraps I won't even know how to tie.

Jamila stands up and wipes the dirt off the seat of her shorts. We're in the garden, one of our favorite spots, but it's not like it used to be. She's about to leave me again, and even though I'm mad at her, I don't want her to go, so

I pick a few raspberries off one of the plants and hand them to her. But she shakes her head and pushes my hand away.

"My *paapa* says people in Ghana aren't really into rabbit food."

Chapter Twenty-Four

FREESTYLE

adj. denoting a contest or version of a sport in which there are few restrictions on the moves or techniques that competitors employ: *Freestyle swimming.*

n. a performance or routine featuring free, un-restricted movement or intended to demonstrate an individual's special skills or style

Nana and Granddad are sitting together on the couch, still cooing over their gardening catalogs. What should they plant—crocuses and tulips or just tulips? What's the big deal? They turn the pages of that catalog like they're made of gold.

"Neva, what you no good?" Granddad asks. He says it without looking at me. Without turning around.

Nana slaps his hand. "That child doesn't know what you're saying. Talking that old talk."

They're sitting there giggling like two teenagers waiting for their friend, me, to join in. But I don't. I can't believe they think everything's okay. It's not.

Mama has her singing and Daddy has Mama and Clay has his Anton and they, Granddad and Nana, have their old jokes and Jamila has her trip. Everybody has something except me.

Jamila pushed my hand away. Part of my brain knows that but another part of me, my heart, wants to act like it didn't happen. How could it happen?

Granddad looks up. "Where's Jamila?"

"She went home."

Granddad nods like that's no big deal. "Probably has a lot to do to get ready for her trip. I sure wish I was going."

"I spoke with her mama," Nana says, looking up at me. "She asked about you."

Nana's watching my face so closely. She's looking straight at me. Like maybe she can see that hole that's just waiting to swallow me up. She can see it behind my eyes.

"Your mama misses you so much," Nana says. "It's not easy for her to be away this summer, but she still has dreams too." She turns toward the window and for a moment it feels like she's someplace else. Like she's not here in the living room with me and Granddad.

Granddad reaches over and strokes her hand with his right index finger, and Nana turns back toward me.

"What about you?" she says, smiling again. "You need something to do today. It's beautiful out."

It used to be I'd squeeze in between my grandparents and have fun with them all day, but now I'm standing over them feeling left out. I never thought I'd feel like this in my own house.

Granddad looks at me too. "You don't have to go out if you don't want to." He bends over toward his pile of old DVDs. "Want to watch a movie with us?"

I know he's trying to help but he can't. Watching *The Shawshank Redemption* for the fifth time isn't going to do it. Besides, I have a meeting to go to.

"Mrs. Giles probably has a lot of kids over at the swim club," I say. "I'll be over there."

"Mrs. Giles," says Nana, smiling. "We're lucky to have her."

I go upstairs to get my bathing suit and towel. I shove my flip-flops into my backpack and think about all the lying I'm doing. My slide away from the truth has been pretty quick and it's getting harder to even remember a day without fibbing. *Fibbing.* That's one of Granddad's words and I use it because it makes me feel better. Of course, a fib is a lie, but according to my dictionary it's typically an unimportant one.

Yeah, cutting out from the swim club to go to a meeting isn't the worst thing in the world. I'm just freestyling. Look at it that way. I don't want to think about what Mama would say if she knew so I avoid looking at my face in my little mirror and keep moving.

I'm doing something for my community and I don't need to feel guilty about it. If I were on trial I could, possibly, be charged with withholding information but that's all. Granddad and Nana are the ones who said I needed something to do today and they're probably very happy to see me go. What's that Nana said when we were in Center City? *If I don't take care of myself nobody else will.*

Chapter Twenty-Five

ALIBI

n. a claim or piece of evidence that one was elsewhere when an act, typically a criminal one, is alleged to have taken place: *She has an alibi for yesterday afternoon.*

The squeals of laughter coming from the swim club don't do anything for me today. Clay's on duty up in the lifeguard's chair but there's no Jamila and no Mrs. Giles. Her assistant is here with some kids I've never seen before.

I'm standing outside the girls' locker room in just the right spot to wave at Clay. I need to make sure he sees me just in case I need proof that I was here. He nods in my direction but turns his attention right back to the few kids in the pool. I lean up against the white walls trying to look nonchalant. You know, real casual. Maybe I'll stay here for five more minutes before I cut out, but then I hear a familiar voice.

"All alone today?" Mrs. Giles asks, flashing me a smile.

I nod. Now my alibi is airtight. Both Clay and Mrs. Giles can say I've been here.

"Actually, I'm not surprised," Mrs. Giles continues. "I suspect I'll see a lot of young people over at the March for Justice meeting." She checks her watch and I check her out. She's not wearing her flip-flops or her whistle today. She's carrying a tote bag filled with flyers and other stuff. "Are you going over?"

Mrs. Giles is going to the meeting. This is too good to be true. Nana and Granddad can't object to my going with her. I don't even have to worry about Clay seeing me leave. Perfect.

The community center is in a church a few blocks away on Baltimore Avenue. I'm walking alongside Mrs. Giles and she's very chatty even when she's stepping over the uneven sidewalks. I didn't know she was born and raised here in West Philly.

"I've been here so long I can remember a time when these tree roots weren't growing all up through the pavement," she laughs. Walking through the neighborhood with her is like walking with royalty.

Royalty: people of royal blood or status; the most successful, famous, or highly regarded members of a particular group

Everybody knows Mrs. Giles.

"I try to do what I can with my hiring at the swim club," she says, "but it's not nearly enough. There's been such a lack of investment in our community for so long."

I nod as we continue along and walk right up to a woman sweeping her sidewalk. She holds her broom still and rubs Mrs. Giles's arm as she looks down at me.

"This has to be Tracey Beane's daughter. Looks just like her."

"Isn't she something? She's always been so sharp," says Mrs. Giles. She shines her electric-lightbulb smile on me again even though she's doing that adult thing I don't understand. Talking about me like I'm not standing right here.

Sharp is what she called me. Is that what I am?

We walk the rest of the way over to the center with me sorting through all the words I keep in my head. But the one I need right now to describe myself doesn't seem to be there.

Anton and another teenager stand outside the community center handing out flyers and encouraging people to come inside. He looks down at the pavement when he sees me but hands a flyer to Mrs. Giles. "I have more than I need already," she says, lifting her tote bag to show him. "But don't forget about Neva."

Anton stammers something I can't hear and hands me about five flyers, way more than I need. He doesn't look directly at me but I can feel his eyes on my back as I pass.

Me and Mrs. Giles step out of the bright sunshine into the cool cavern of the church. It's dimmer in here than it is outside, but that doesn't stamp out the energy coming from all the people sitting on folding chairs and talking. A man who looks like Michelle hands Mrs. Giles a pamphlet and then gives me another copy of the March for Justice flyer. Is this Michelle's daddy, Mr. Overton?

At first, I think this is just one big meeting but it's actually a bunch of smaller meetings going on in this one huge room. Mrs. Giles takes it all in before another man waves her over to the group talking about jobs. She gestures for me to sit down with her, but I see Michelle over in the corner with a group of older kids.

"That's the Youth Committee," the man says. "Go on over, if you want."

Michelle's back is to me so she doesn't see me walk over but she's definitely the one in charge. Even some adults are leaning over to listen.

"Sunday's march isn't about any one issue," she says.

"It's about all the things impacting our community—immigration, jobs, affordable housing . . ."

I look around to check out the other kids. Lots of cool piercings and tattoos but nobody cares about how anybody looks. There's something else going on here. It feels like . . . like electricity.

Yeah. There's an electric current that I can almost see jumping from person to person. And it doesn't skip over me either. It races up my spine and guides my eyes up to the top of the church's tall stone walls. All the way up to the stained glass windows that spread the outside light so it falls back onto the church floor in smooth, colorful patterns. The light is beautiful. Just like Michelle.

"You all know I like to do my clothes thing," she says.

She's making everybody laugh so easily with her smooth, comfortable style.

"It's fun to try things out but Sunday should be all about comfort." She holds up one leg and wags her index finger back and forth as she points down to her wedges. "You will not see me in these. Wear comfortable shoes and clothing."

So, she's just trying different styles out with her clothes? She's so much more sophisticated than me in every way.

Michelle pauses and a couple of kids ask questions about the route.

"We'll meet at city hall and then head up the Ben Franklin—"

Michelle sees me and stops. She looks me up and down before her face breaks into a smile. "Everybody knows Clay Beane, right? Well, he's not here today but his sister, Neva, is."

Michelle points at me and now I'm on the spot. Every single head turns to look and my right hand goes straight up to twist my hair. I'm supposed to say something, but what?

"You got it, little sis," a guy says, nodding. He's older than me but he wants to hear what I have to say?

I turn around frantically looking for Mrs. Giles but I don't see her. I think about the homeless people on Baltimore Avenue and Anton's brother in prison but I don't have the words to really talk about those things. Somehow, the words I know don't seem like enough.

"I'm new to all this." That's what comes out.

The guy in front of me smiles and even in the soft light I see his eyes light up.

"So, I'm here to find out more about the march."

"Know how to be around the police," he answers. "That's the most important thing."

"I've never really been around the police."

"Tell her about detractors," somebody else says. "She needs to know how to handle herself around them too."

Detractors? Who are they? The people who shoved Clay around at the rally he went to?

"What do I do if somebody gets in my face?" I ask, and several people nod their heads.

"She's asking good questions," another voice calls out. "That's real smart."

I don't know how smart it is 'cause I'm feeling like I'm in over my head again.

"Keep asking questions. That's a good place to start."

I turn around again to search for Mrs. Giles but I still don't see her. Who I do see is our neighbor Mr. Charles and he's walking right over to me.

"Neva, Mrs. Giles got a call and she had to leave," he says in a calm voice, "but don't worry, she asked me to walk you home." He looks me dead in my face but he doesn't ask if Granddad knows I'm here.

"A call?"

"Now, don't you worry," he says. "Nothing happened to Clay but somebody broke their leg or something over at the pool."

Somebody broke their leg? How could that happen?

Michelle is talking about how kids should only go to

the march with their parents or guardians. Well, my parents are in another country and my guardians don't even know I'm here.

Mr. Charles guides me to the door where Michelle's father is standing with Anton.

"Thanks for coming," Mr. Overton says. "It's an honor to have Clay's sister down with us. He's doing a lot of important work."

Mr. Charles nods and opens the door for me.

"See you Sunday," says Mr. Overton.

Chapter Twenty-six

BETRAYAL

n. treachery; the action of exposing one's country, one's group, or a person to danger or distress by a disloyal act: *His friends were shocked by his betrayal.*

Mr. Charles tries to make small talk on the way home but I can't laugh at his trolley jokes. Who cares about the whooshing sound the trolley cars make when they glide through the neighborhood? What I really want to do is jump on one and ride it away from here.

How can things change so dramatically from one second to the next? For one sweet moment Michelle respected me and all those other kids wanted to hear what I had to say. Now I'm walking straight into big, big trouble. Today wasn't supposed to roll out like this.

"I heard your parents' tour is going very well," says Mr. Charles. "You should be proud of them."

I can't even try to fix my face into a smile. We're approaching our block and I'm wondering if there's any way I can ditch Mr. Charles. I could say I forgot something at the community center. He won't walk me back over there, right?

"Charles, is that you?" shouts Granddad. "How'd you make it over to the swim club before us?" Granddad and Nana are hurrying down the street toward us.

"What are you talking about?" says Mr. Charles.

"Jamila fell at the pool and broke something," says Granddad, looking from me to Mr. Charles and back to me again. "Clay didn't see you, Neva, in all the confusion, so he asked us to come find you 'cause he thought you'd be upset."

"What?" I say, shaking my head and blinking 'cause I'm not sure I heard him right. Jamila was all right when I saw her this morning.

"Oh, so that's what happened," says Mr. Charles, putting his hand on his forehead. "Mrs. Giles had to leave us at the meeting—"

"Stop right there," says Granddad. "What meeting?"

Mr. Charles looks at me and moves his hand slowly down his face from his forehead to his mouth, but it's too late.

I take a deep breath and hum. I'm humming because I don't trust my voice.

"Neva?" I hear Nana say.

I only hear it because I'm looking down at the prickly pear cactus growing in our neighbor's garden. Its egg yolk–colored flowers are beautiful but they're surrounded by the plant's sharp spines. I've often wondered how it would feel if you lost your balance and fell on the cactus. Now I know.

"You weren't there when Jamila got hurt, were you?" she asks.

I shake my head but I still don't dare to meet Nana's gaze. It's bad enough feeling her eyes bore into my head.

Nobody says anything until I break the awful silence. "I went to the community meeting for the march," I finally whisper.

"Without permission," Nana says. Her voice is low like mine but there's something else in it. Something way past hurt. It's betrayal. I spell it out in my head but I don't dare get too close to that word.

"I was with Mrs. Giles." I say her name hoping it will work its usual magic, but my grandparents don't respond. "And Mr. Charles walked me home."

"You were there too?" Granddad asks, turning to Mr. Charles. "Funny, you didn't say anything to me about it."

"There's nothing funny about any of this," says Nana. "Geneva, we're responsible for you while your parents are away. Why are you making this so hard?"

I open my mouth to apologize but one look at her face makes me close it again. No amount of humming is going to make this right.

I'm not trying to make her life hard. I'm not. So why have I made a mess of everything again? I look at Granddad and he shakes his head. Even he doesn't know what to say. We all just stand there on the cracked side-walk and watch Nana turn and slowly walk away.

Chapter Twenty-Seven

BROKEN

adj. 1. having been fractured or damaged and no longer in working order *2.* (of a person) having given up all hope; despairing: *A broken spirit.*

"Well, I have to get over to the hospital," says Mr. Charles. He gives me a weak smile but avoids making eye contact with Granddad.

I brace myself for what's coming next, but Granddad's quiet. We walk to our house and there's no sign of Nana in the garden or on the porch.

"She's probably in the backyard," says Granddad, going around the side of the house to find her.

I'm rooted to one spot in our garden and I stand there trying to push that feeling of being swallowed up away. Nana confided in me because there was a bond between us. She told me how Clay made her feel and she never

ever thought I'd do anything like that. Now that bond is broken.

My neck is tightening up like it does before I get a bad headache. I look down at the raspberries and wish I had the power to turn back time. I'd turn it back to this morning when I was here with Jamila. Why couldn't I just be happy for her? Maybe then she would have taken the raspberries from me and none of this would have happened.

Granddad comes slowly back around our house and puts his hands on my shoulders.

"I didn't mean to . . ." I say, searching his face for a clue of how Nana's doing.

"She's . . . she's upset," he says. "We should give her some time to herself."

"She's mad, isn't she?"

"She's more worried than mad," Granddad says, but I shake my head no.

"She's mad, Granddad, and I know why. She told me how Clay made her feel. And I . . . I did the same thing."

Granddad purses his lips and his grip tightens on my shoulders.

"She feels like everybody takes her for granted and that's what I did." I feel the tears coming but I don't try to stop them. "I did it without thinking about her."

Granddad pauses before he speaks. "There's been a lot of tension in our house," he sighs. "Don't work yourself up into a migraine."

He says that but it's too late. Already, my head feels squeezed like a band is tightening around it. I close my eyes hoping that will stave off the dizziness.

I hurt Nana. It doesn't matter that I didn't mean to. My closed eyes don't make me feel any better. There's nothing I can do to avoid the truth now.

"All of this happened because I'm mad, Granddad. And . . . I don't know what to do with it."

"Is that what you've been feeling?"

"I guess so." My voice cracks on that last word and I look up at him.

Granddad's mouth opens but nothing comes out. He looks up at our house as if he wishes the front porch could reach out and hug us.

"You been thinking about this a lot," he says.

"Yeah," I say, leaning into his chest. "I'm mad because everything's changing."

"We're here to take care of you. That hasn't changed," he whispers. "Let's get you upstairs."

He leads me through the garden and I know I'm in for a bad, bad headache. The earthy smells I usually love just make me feel sick now. It's only a few steps to the front porch but I'm shriveled up like a green bean that's been left on the vine too long when I hear somebody running toward us. I don't see him but the scent of heat mixed with sweat and chlorine tells me it's Clay.

"Neva," he yells. "Did you hear about Jamila?"

"Don't upset her now," says Granddad. "She's having one of her headaches."

"What happened?" I ask.

Clay lowers his voice. "She was running with some new kids around the big pool and slipped," he says. "She broke her foot *and* her ankle."

Jamila running? She knows that's not allowed. She never does that. I ask myself why she would act out, but I know the answer.

"She probably won't be going on her trip," says Clay, and I squeeze my eyes shut again.

The dictionary inside my head has been replaced by a drummer. A mad woman drummer who's not holding back. She's playing the drums and crashing cymbals with all her might. Thump, thump, clash. Thump, thump, clash. Thump, thump, clash.

Chapter Twenty-Eight

CUDDLE

v. to hold close in one's arms as a way of showing love or affection; to hug tenderly: *He cuddles the baby.*

I wake up hours later in my darkened bedroom. My headache is gone. The house is quiet. Someone has taken care of me. There's no doubt about that. The evening is warm and I'm so glad I can smell things again without feeling like I'm going to throw up. I can even listen to the birds settling in on the ledge outside my window without their sounds piercing my skull.

Granddad knocks and sticks his head in my room. "Feeling better?" he asks.

I nod and he steps in with some crackers and a plastic cup. "Here, at least drink the water."

He watches me eat all the crackers and smiles when I drain the water in the cup.

"Feel good enough to take a walk? Some fresh air may do you good," he says.

"How's Nana?" I ask.

"She's still resting so let's be quiet on our way out."

Granddad's quiet lasts all the way from our house through the tangle of traffic as we make our way over to Civic Center Boulevard. He didn't tell me we were going to the hospital.

"Don't worry," he says. "I'm not checking you in." I don't laugh at his joke but he still squeezes my hand in his.

He nods to people we pass at the entrance and shows his ID at the front desk before signing me in as his guest. We step off the busy elevator into the long, beige hallway and I see a sign directing volunteer cuddlers into a quiet room with rocking chairs.

"Is this where you and Mr. Charles volunteer?"

"Mm-hmm," he says. "This is where I come to gain perspective on things."

"Mr. Robinson," a nurse says. "Mr. Charles was here earlier but we weren't expecting you tonight."

"I know it's not my usual shift but I wanted my granddaughter to experience this," he says, opening his arms wide.

The nurse smiles like she knows exactly what he's talking about. Granddad ushers me into the cuddlers' room and takes a seat in a rocker.

"You're going to hold a baby now?" I ask.

"There's no telling when a little one may need attention, Neva. Volunteers are needed at all times, day and night."

"But why are—"

"Shhh," he says, motioning me to the rocker next to his. "You have to be calm within yourself to be a good cuddler."

The nurse comes back but this time she has a tiny baby in her arms. "Her name is Zamaya," she says as Granddad reaches up for the baby. "She wasn't abandoned but she was low-weight at birth. Her parents are doing the best they can but they can't spend all their time here holding her."

The nurse stands at the door and watches my granddad touch Zamaya's cheek before she smiles and leaves. Granddad gives Zamaya her bottle and rocks gently in the wooden chair.

"Your mama and daddy love you to death," he says.

I'm not sure if he's talking to me or the baby until he goes on.

"They never would have gone away this summer if

they didn't know how much Nana and I love you and that we'd do everything we can to support you. Especially Nana. She's the real backbone of the family. But let's not talk about her now. Let's talk about me."

He's looking down at Zamaya. Maybe that makes it easier to say these things.

"Sometimes I don't know what to do and I come off a little too gruff," he says. "But it's only because I care about you that I'm afraid for you. And now that I'm saying this out loud, I think maybe that's not right. Maybe I'm afraid of you. Afraid that you'll grow up too soon and move away from me. But one of the things I've learned from holding these babies is that you have to be calm to do them any good. They pick up energy from you and they respond to it. Sort of like what's been happening between me and you." Granddad pauses and looks up at me. "So, what I'm saying, Neva, is let's be calm together."

He takes the empty bottle out of Zamaya's mouth, places her on his shoulder, and gently pats her back. She wiggles her feet and hands and makes little burping sounds.

Granddad smiles and hands Zamaya over to me. "Wanna try?" he asks.

Chapter Twenty-Nine

EMPATHY

n. 1. the ability to understand and share the feelings of another *2.* the imaginative experiencing of feelings, thoughts, or attitudes: *The nurse was filled with empathy for her patients.*

It's totally dark when Granddad and I push through our house's little gate and step into our garden, but the porch light is on and it casts a soft glow over the front of our house. It doesn't feel that much different from the cuddlers' room at the hospital. This is how home should feel all the time.

Granddad unlocks the front door and we see Nana sitting all alone at the dining room table. She's slumped a little in her chair and her head falls forward every few seconds before she pulls it back up, but she still manages to look elegant.

"Nana, what time is it? You should be in bed."

I'm standing next to her at the table but Granddad lingers at the foot of the stairs.

Nana squeezes my hand and then pats it. "How's your head?" she asks, getting up.

"Much better."

"That's good." She takes a few seconds to smooth the front of her blouse. "Those headaches are awful."

"Did you see my note?" asks Granddad. "We were over at the hospital."

Nana nods and puts her arm around me. "I know you just got in, but I feel like sitting outside. Want to join me?"

"I'll be upstairs," says Granddad, moving aside so we can pass him.

Me and Nana sit on the green rattan love seat for a few seconds not saying anything. She hums softly and I think about how it would feel to stay like this forever, but that would be too easy. I'm not a baby anymore. I should stop acting like one.

"Are you sure that light isn't bothering you?" she asks, looking up at the porch ceiling. I can't stand light when I'm in the grips of a headache but my head doesn't hurt anymore, and anyway I don't want to use that as an excuse.

"Nana, I'm sorry . . ."

"I know you are," she says.

"We, me and Clay—"

"Clay and I," she interrupts, and I nod.

"Clay and I tiptoe around Granddad but we expect you to be nice all the time. It isn't fair."

"You can't speak for Clay, Neva. Just speak for yourself," she says, looking straight at me in that way she has of looking deep inside my heart. It's not the way she would look at me if she thought I was still a little girl. It's that new way she's been looking at me since my body and everything else started changing.

"You told me how you felt disrespected but I didn't really know what that was like until I felt it myself. I felt like nobody cared about me so I had to prove something. To myself, mainly." Nana nods her head. Not in agreement but to let me know she's listening to me. "And when I got to that meeting people wanted to hear what I had to say, but I didn't really know what to do with myself."

"Why do you feel you have to do something with yourself?"

"I don't know." I shrug, looking out at the shadows in the garden. "It's hard to explain. I mean, I know I'm great, but sometimes I don't know if that's enough . . . compared to other people."

"You know you're great, Neva. You're already ahead of the game. You don't need to do or be anything else."

"That's what Mama says too."

"Your mama's called three times today. Twice while you were sleeping and once while you were out," Nana says. "She's ready to cut the tour short."

I'd thought I wanted to hear those words but now they sound selfish. I can't ask Mama to give up her dream. To walk away from what she needs.

"Mama can't leave the tour, Nana. She shouldn't do that."

"Isn't that what you wanted?"

"No . . . I mean, yes . . . I mean, I did want it, but I don't want it now."

"Knowing what you really want is hard," she says, "but you always question things, Neva. And that's good. You question things and you figure them out. You didn't go about this in the right way but you found that spark that I was afraid you'd lost."

"You could see that?"

Nana nods. "You're not the only girl to go through that. And even when you're an adult you can suffer bouts of insecurity." Nana tilts her head. "You have no idea how hard Granddad and I had to work to get your mama to feel okay about going away for the summer. She didn't want to be away from you. But we've all seen how her eyes light up when she's singing, right? How could we let her pass that up?"

"I'm glad she didn't."

"Do you really mean that?"

I look out into our half-lit garden and picture Mama standing on a stage in front of an audience. Her eyes are closed but her mouth and her whole body are open. She's rapturous. That's the word that pops into my head.

Rapturous: characterized by, feeling, or expressing great pleasure or enthusiasm

Singing is Mama's way of prancing. She needs that just as much as I do.

"Daddy said Mama's on fire, Nana, on fire. She can't give that up."

Nana grins and stands up. "No, she shouldn't." She moves quickly to open the screen door. "But if you really don't want her to leave the tour we better get ahold of her before she tells Ms. G she's quitting. Your daddy told me all you-know-what will break loose if that happens."

Nana's inside the house in two seconds, calling up the stairs. "What time is it in Europe, Dexter? Where's my phone?"

Chapter Thirty

STRENGTH

n. 1. the quality or state of being physically strong: *Weightlifting can build up your strength. 2.* the capacity of an object, substance, or person to withstand great force or pressure, as in the emotional or mental qualities necessary in dealing with situations or events that are distressing

It's eleven thirty at night here in Philly, five thirty a.m. in Amsterdam. Nana's disappeared into her bedroom, so I go into mine to send Mama a message.

Please don't quit, Mama. Ms. G needs you.

Out in the hallway I hear Nana and Granddad bad-mouthing their phones. "These darn things never work when you need them," Granddad says.

"You're pushing too many keys, Dexter. Here, let me do it."

"We wouldn't be in this fix if you kept your phone charged, Cecily."

I stick my head out my door. They'd be funny if they weren't wasting time.

Granddad sees me and yells, "Neva . . . Clay . . . somebody . . . call your mama."

Granddad's a sight in his blue plaid bathrobe, short white socks, and leather slippers, but he has one arm tenderly draped over Nana's shoulders. I have no idea why he's wearing socks at night in the summertime, but it doesn't really matter.

Clay's door pops open and he leans over the railing. "What's going on?" he asks. "I thought you all were down for the night."

"Nobody's lying down while your mama's career's on the line," says Granddad. "We gotta get to her before she quits."

My phone rings and I retreat back into my room to pick it up.

"Neva, I'm so sorry I'm not there," says Mama. "How are you feeling?"

"I'm fine, Mama. Just don't quit."

There's silence for a few seconds and I imagine Mama's face. Furrowed brows and tight lips. Her confused look.

"I'm worried about you, sweetie. I know this summer's been hard. What's really going on?"

"I was afraid of losing myself."

"Oh, baby . . ." Mama gulps like the wind's been kicked out of her. "You're too strong for that."

She's talking about strength. That's the real magic word. That's the thing I'd lost sight of in myself.

"Mama?"

It sounds like she's blowing her nose. Is she crying?

"I'm coming home," she says. "It's not worth this."

"I said I WAS afraid but I'm not anymore."

"Neva—"

"I had a bout of insecurity, that's all. I'm okay now."

"A bout of insecurity?" Mama makes a weird noise like a half laugh, half sniffle. "I see you've been reading Nana's magazines again."

"We talked about it, me and Nana," I say.

"Nana and I."

"Yeah. It's all confused, but I was afraid I couldn't be myself without you, but then I found what everybody else knew was in me all the time."

"That's a mouthful. I'm not sure I follow."

Mama's not making her gasping sounds anymore so I tell her about that feeling of falling down into a deep hole, stressing that I *used to have* those feelings. I don't have them anymore even though I'm shaking a little bit because I haven't eaten much since my headache went away.

"You never mentioned this deep hole before," she says. "But I've gone through something like that too. I should be there with you."

"What about Ms. G?"

"I'm more worried about you and Clay—"

"Clay's fine—"

"That's not for you to say," Mama says. "And the girl across the street. What's her name, Michelle?"

"Why's everybody so worried about Michelle? Every time her name comes up . . ."

Mama sighs. "Michelle knows her strength and she's not afraid to show it. That's a very powerful thing."

Mama doesn't say anything for a few more seconds but then adds, "Now I'm suffering a bout of insecurity. Maybe I'm fooling myself. Leaving my kids to try to sing at this stage . . ."

Mama afraid? I think about all the times I needed encouragement and how she handled it. She always made me feel better with a song. So I do the same for her even though my throat is dry and my voice isn't half as beautiful as hers.

I start by humming and then I snap the fingers of my left hand real close to the phone so she can hear it.

Mama giggles and sighs 'cause she knows what's coming. "Go ahead, baby, sing me a song."

"Mama, oh, Mama. Please don't quit now," I croon in a soft, low voice. "You have just got to sing your song, sing your song, sing your song . . ."

Chapter Thirty-One

SOAPBOX

n. a box or crate used as a makeshift stand by a public speaker; a thing that provides an opportunity for someone to air their views publicly: *His blog was his soapbox.*

The last notes of my serenade are still in my throat when I put my phone down and turn around to find Clay standing at my door.

"Not only do you look like Mama," he says, "you sound like her too."

I clear my throat because I don't know how much of my conversation he heard and I feel a little exposed. Sort of the same way I did when he found me admiring myself in the mirror. But he's not laughing this time and I'm not afraid to look him in the eye.

"I told her we're okay so she shouldn't quit—"

"I know, I heard the *Clay's fine* part." He raises his voice in a fake imitation of how I talk, but I don't sound like that at all and he knows it.

Clay straightens the multicolored quilt on my bed and sits down with his head in his hands. "I was hoping they'd come home early. Like tomorrow and get me off punishment so I can go to the march. I know I can reason with them."

"What about Nana? She's the one who grounded you."

"I know but Dad can overrule her."

"Really? Is that what you think?"

There's a sharpness in my voice that neither of us expected. Clay lifts his head and frowns at me.

"I should be at that march," he says. "Everything that's going on—"

"There's a lot going on here too, Clay. You don't know how much you hurt Nana."

"Dang," he sighs. "How many times do I have to apologize?"

"You apologized but did you really mean it?" I'm sounding a little high and mighty but he needs to hear this. "How would you feel if—"

"Oh, you've been hanging with Michelle so now you've got your own little soapbox."

"I don't know about a soapbox but I'm wondering why you didn't forge Granddad's name."

Clay wrinkles his eyebrows together in that way

everyone in this family does when they're confused. He's so sensitive about some things. Why can't he get this?

I turn away and check the time on my phone because the look on my brother's face tells me he needs a few seconds of privacy.

"You think I have it all together," Clay says from behind me. "But, okay, maybe I don't."

I don't know what to say to that so I just keep fiddling with my phone until the silence between us is shattered by Granddad's voice in the background. It's past midnight but he always shouts when he's on a long-distance call.

"He doesn't really need a phone," says Clay. "People in Europe can hear him just fine without it."

"I know all of West Philly sure can."

We laugh a little and I tell Clay how Mr. Charles came over to check on us the other night.

"Mr. Charles is all right," says Clay, standing up and stretching. He twists his lips into a sheepish grin. That's the only word for how he looks.

Sheepish: showing embarrassment from shame or a lack of self-confidence

"I would say see you in the morning," he says. "But it's morning already."

It's still dark outside but Clay and I are cool again. That's in itself a form of light.

Chapter Thirty-Two

RECOGNITION

n. 1. identification of someone or something from previous encounters or knowledge *2.* acknowledgment of something's existence, validity, or legality: *Her recognition of the truth made all the difference.*

It's morning but I don't leap out of bed like I do when I know Jamila's waiting for me. Instead, I stretch a few times, hoping the empty spot in my chest will go away, but it doesn't move even one inch on its own. I close my eyes and relive last night's conversations with Mama and Clay. They weren't so hard so I hope being honest with Jamila won't be either.

I'm sorry you're hurt. Be over after breakfast. That's the message I send my girl before going down to eat.

Granddad's at the table but he's still in his nightclothes.

Nightclothes as in pajamas. Not what anybody would wear to go out clubbing. He looks a little disheveled.

Disheveled: untidy

That's not usually his style.

"Excuse my attire, Baby Girl." He peeks at me over the top of his newspaper and I can tell from his eyes that he's suppressing a smile. "I'm not used to pulling these all-nighters."

Technically it wasn't an all-nighter since as far as I know, we were all quieted down by one a.m., but I don't correct him. He doesn't look that bad and anyway, what's the big deal?

Clay comes out of the kitchen with a plate of pancakes in each hand. He places one plate in front of me and gives the other to Granddad. He turns right back around and disappears into the kitchen again before I can say anything.

"Why don't you go sit down," I hear him say to Nana. "I got these last two plates."

So, we're all going to just sit here and eat and act like it's totally normal for Clay to make breakfast? I could say something smart about it, but I don't.

"How'd everybody sleep?" Nana asks, sipping her hibiscus tea.

"Like a baby?" says Granddad, winking at me.

"Are you going over to Jamila's?" Clay asks. "She'll be glad to see you."

I hope that's true but he doesn't know what happened between us. He didn't see us in the garden struggling with the raspberries. Jamila broke her foot *and* her ankle and I had the worst headache of my life. We tried to hide our emotions but they found a way out like they always do.

Chapter Thirty-Three

SPURN

v. reject with disdain or contempt: *She spurned their invitation to dance with a flick of her wrist.*

It must have rained last night because the honey fragrance of mint slaps me in the face when I open the screen door and step out onto our front porch. The plants are taller too and the sidewalk is more wet than it would be just from the morning dew.

I jump down into our garden and fill a baggie with as much mint as it will hold but I ignore the raspberries that are sitting right there looking at me. They're ripe but I leave them on the vine.

I ride my bike over to Jamila's, rehearsing what I'm going to say:

I'm sorry about your foot and ankle. Do they hurt?

That's totally stupid and phony. Of course I heard about what happened. Clay was on duty at the swim club when she fell. How about:

You broke your foot and your ankle? Are you still going to Ghana?

That's not right either. It sounds like I'm gloating and I'm not.

I pedal faster, thinking I can maybe get my brain to work faster too. I ride right up to Jamila's daddy and her auntie standing on the sidewalk in front of her family's dark blue Volvo.

"Eh-heh, you remember Neva?" Mr. Mensah says to his older sister.

"Ahh, of course. Isn't she the one Jamila is always talking about?"

"I'm afraid your friend is not doing so well," Mr. Mensah says, turning to me and shaking his head.

"Is it bad?"

"Hmm . . . it could be worse," he says, putting one hand over his heart, "but the accident . . . our trip."

"She had her heart set on it. We all did," says Jamila's auntie. "Now . . ."

I don't know what to say so I hold up my little baggie and Mr. Mensah smiles and points toward the back of the house.

"She's in the backyard," he says.

The Mensah backyard is one of my favorite places but there's no joy in it this morning. The colorful mural and the Ghanaian flag are still here but Jamila's sitting in one of the chairs at the little café table with her outstretched right leg resting across a second chair. Most of her right foot and leg are in a cast. She's fiddling with her cell, but as of the last time I checked she still hasn't responded to my message.

She doesn't know I'm here or maybe she does and she doesn't want to see me. She probably heard me talking with her daddy but she hasn't turned around.

I clear my throat and wait a second before saying anything.

"Hey." I open the little gate that closes off the yard from the side of their house.

"Hey," she says. She shifts her outstretched leg but she doesn't lift it off the second chair. Maybe she can't because of the cast?

"Clay told me what happened," I say, walking over to where she's sitting. "Does it hurt?"

"Not really," she says, shrugging and rolling her eyes.

"I'm sorry—"

"It hurt when I first tried to walk on it," she continues, cutting me off. "Before I got the cast, but not now."

"That's good. How long will you be in it?"

"Four or five weeks," she says, still looking down at her phone. "It's a drag 'cause I can't get it wet—"

"I guess that means no swimming." The sentence comes out of my mouth and I immediately regret it. She can't even walk. I look over at her red bike chained to the fence. She can't ride a bike now either. She's probably not eager to go back over to the swim club anyway.

Jamila rolls her eyes again. "And the doctor said it may start to itch . . ."

I'm standing by the table 'cause there's no place for me to sit. "Want something to drink? Some tea?" I nod toward her house. "I brought some mint."

"I don't really feel like it," she says, but Mrs. Mensah calls out the kitchen window.

"Hi, Neva. Is that mint you have with you?"

"Oh, who cares," I hear Jamila say as I walk over to their back door.

Her mama steps outside and her eyes shift from her daughter to me and back to her daughter again. There's a look like a big question mark on her face but she doesn't ask us what's going on.

"How are you feeling this morning?" Mrs. Mensah asks. "Headache gone?"

How does she know that? She's not old enough to be psychic like Granddad and Nana.

"Tracey said it was one of your worst. She called me last night because she was so worried about you."

"Neva's mama called you from Europe?" Jamila asks, turning around.

"Mm-hmm. She asked us to check in on them, but, of course, we were busy here."

"Your headache must have been bad," Jamila says, looking at me. "I mean, for your mama to call all the way from Amsterdam."

"It was, but it's over. I'm back to normal now."

"You mean you're back to your political stuff?"

"Political stuff?" asks Mrs. Mensah. "I didn't know you were politically active."

"She's organizing that march everybody's talking about," says Jamila, avoiding my eyes and talking a little too loud.

"No, I'm not. I haven't even asked my grandparents if I can go."

"Well, that's not what you said yesterday. Yesterday you said you were going."

I said a lot of things yesterday. Things I wish I hadn't but Jamila remembers them all and she's not about to let me forget.

"I'm sure she'll get her parents' approval before she gets more involved, sweetie. Right, Neva?" Mrs. Mensah turns to me. "You'll talk with them about it?"

I nod meekly. I haven't thought much about the march with everything else going on but it's scheduled for Sunday and Michelle and her daddy are expecting me or Clay or both of us to show.

Jamila sits at the table looking down at her cell even though her mama tries to make conversation. She plays me off like I'm not even there.

"Well, I'm going over to the swim—" I stop myself before the word *club* comes out, but it's too late.

Jamila looks up and her mouth is pinched. "Going skinny-dipping with Michelle?" she asks.

I've never been smacked in the face but Jamila's question stings like the back of a hand on my cheek. Her question hangs over the little café table, forcing me to step back.

"Where did that come from?" Mrs. Mensah says, frowning at her daughter. "I don't like how you sound, Jamila."

Mrs. Mensah may not know where that voice came from but I do. And there's nothing I can say right now to make it go away.

Chapter Thirty-Four

REFUGE

n. 1. a condition of being safe or sheltered from pursuit, danger, or trouble: *He was forced to take refuge in the French embassy.* *2.* something providing shelter: *The family came to be seen as a refuge from a harsh world.*

"Back so soon?" asks Granddad when I open the screen door and step through the vestibule. "I didn't think we'd see you for the rest of the day."

He and Nana are sitting in the living room and it feels like I'm interrupting something. I take my old spot between them on the couch hoping their warmth will lessen the sting of Jamila's put-down.

"What's wrong?" says Nana, stroking my hair. She has a funny way of doing it. She's sort of twisting my twists and patting them down at the same time. "Is Jamila all right?"

"I don't know," I say, and Nana's hand comes to a dead stop. "She's mad at me."

"Tell us what happened," Nana says, shifting over on the couch as I give a blow-by-blow replay of everything.

"She was so looking forward to that trip," Nana says. "Now she's lost that and she thinks she's lost you too."

Granddad nods in agreement. "Jamila's a sweetheart. She'll come around, but I can see how she'd be a little jealous of Michelle. My buddy Charles tells me she's pretty sharp."

"You like Michelle now?" I stare at Granddad. "I thought you hated her."

"I didn't really know anything about the young lady."

"But you judged her because of how she dresses."

"Well . . ."

Granddad looks over my head to Nana for help.

"We were wrong about Michelle," says Nana, folding her hands in her lap. "You see how easy it is to make assumptions about people? I certainly should have known better."

"Charles speaks very highly of her and her family," Granddad adds, yawning.

I never told them about Michelle leaving me at the library, but now's not the time to bring that up.

"You need a nap," is what I say.

"Well, we ended up calling your mama and daddy at— What time was that, Cecily?"

"I don't know. Must have been after two," says Nana. "Your mama says you helped her figure things out, Neva. You have quite some power."

I don't know if Mama told them about my serenade but Nana and Granddad don't press me to find out exactly what I did.

"It's not like your parents aren't proud of what you and Clay are trying to do," Granddad says. "Your political work, but they're worried about you. Especially while they're not here."

You mean you're back to your political stuff? Jamila's question from this morning rings in my ears. *Political.* It's starting to feel like that word refers to just about everything.

"Well, your daddy called back just a little while ago and said it's okay for you and Clay to go to the march if somebody, an adult, goes with you."

Granddad's voice is light and breezy but I just snuggle back down in between him and Nana. I don't know if I got involved with the march for the right reasons.

We've only been quiet for a few minutes when Nana

starts to snore. She's not loud like an ugly ringtone on somebody's cell. Her snore is soft. More like a kitten's purring.

"I'm not sure if I really want to go to the march, Granddad. Will you and Nana be there?"

"Me and Charles definitely, but I'm not sure about your grandmother. It's not that she doesn't want to go, but, well, you're not the only one growing up, Neva. We're all getting older. She doesn't think she's up to it and she's struggling with that."

Granddad lifts his right hand to smooth the wild white hairs arching out from his dark eyebrows. He doesn't shape them and I can't even imagine what he'd look like if he did. But his eyebrows were probably all dark at some point. Like, a long time ago. The thing is I never thought about what growing up means for people who are already grown.

Chapter Thirty-Five

ELUCIDATE

v. 1. to make lucid or clear; to throw light upon *2.* to provide clarification; to explain: *The doctor will elucidate your medical problems in his report.*

Clay bounds into the house and heads straight for the kitchen. He's finished work for the day and is hungry, as usual.

"Did you hear the news?" he asks, talking into the refrigerator rather than directly to me. "Mama and Dad said we can go to the march."

I shrug but I don't say anything. My thoughts about the march are all tied up with needing to show out. I still don't know if I got involved because I really want to. And then there's the police and the detractors stuff. And on top of that, I'm still digesting what Granddad said about growing older. How everybody's body keeps changing.

I don't even want to think about what my body will put me through next.

"You don't look too happy," Clay says when he finally turns around. "What's wrong?"

"Everything," I say. "Jamila's mad at me, and the march . . . It makes me a little nervous, Clay. Remember what happened at the one you went to?"

Clay turns back to the refrigerator and pulls out the pitcher of iced tea. We haven't talked about how scared he looked when he got home that night. He pours a glass for me and nods toward the little kitchen table.

"You need to be prepared. That's what I learned. I could help you with that," he says before changing the topic. "Look, you probably don't know this, but Michelle told me everybody liked you at the meeting. Very real. That's how they described you."

"That sounds kind of like I was acting but I wasn't, Clay. I've never been around the police before."

"I know. I'm with you," he says, scratching his neck. "Michelle thinks you would be very effective out front—"

"Me out front? She never asked me."

"Don't do it unless it's something that feels right to you," says Clay. "If that's the case, we'll have to talk with Mr. Overton and Granddad about how you should handle yourself."

"Michelle didn't even ask me," I repeat before going on to tell Clay about Michelle leaving me at the library. "And she hasn't called me since then."

Clay takes a long drink from his glass and sets it back down on the table carefully.

"We need folk like Michelle," he says. "She's doing good things. And sometimes when you're totally focused . . . well, just look what I did to Nana. I can't really criticize Michelle."

"But how do you deal with her?"

Clay takes his time answering this question too. "I've been involved with the community long before Michelle came along. And, to be honest, I was pissed when folks in this house tried to say I was only into the march because of her. Think about that for a minute." Clay folds his arms across his chest and pauses for a few seconds. "But I'm over that 'cause there's no question for me I'm doing the right thing, but you have to decide for yourself."

"I don't like anybody making decisions for me, Clay. I have to be in charge of what I do."

"Tell me something I don't know," he says, smiling. "I'll talk to Michelle. She should put Anton on the front line."

"You'd feel better with him there, right? You're sorta his big brother."

201

"Well, he really misses his real brother," says Clay. "My man's kind of lonely."

"Is that why he comes over here all the time?"

"That and he gets a little kick out of you." Clay rests his chin on his hand. "What, you didn't know that?"

I shrug before answering, "I thought he liked Michelle but Nana saw something else."

"Oh, Lord," Clay says, shaking his head. "I don't have to guess how that went down."

"It wasn't that bad," I say, laughing. "Anton's nice but I'm not thinking about him like that."

"My advice?" Clay says. "Do nothing. Just, you know, keep on being friends."

"Like you and Michelle?"

Clay purses his lips and nods, but I'm not sure if that's all there is to him and Michelle. I don't want to be a pain in the neck so I let it go.

"Do you know Anton's brother?"

Clay nods again. "Yeah. That's one reason why I keep an eye on my man."

"Is the other reason because you wish you had a brother instead of a sister?"

"What?" Clay says without missing a beat. "And miss hanging with you?" He strikes a few poses and we both laugh again. "By the way," he says, stroking the few hairs on his chin. "Guys do that too. I tore that mirror up when my beard first started coming in."

Clay extends his legs out in front of him and stretches his arms over his head.

"You can talk to Michelle about Anton," I say, "but let me talk to her about me."

My brother nods and pours us each another round of iced tea as I tell him about cuddling with Granddad and Zamaya.

"There're lots of ways to show strength, Neva. Lots of ways."

Chapter Thirty-six

POWER

n. l. the capacity or ability to direct or influence the behavior of others or the course of events: *She had me under her power.* *2.* physical strength and force by something or someone: *The power of the storm.* *3.* energy that is produced by mechanical, electrical, or other means and used to operate a device

Nana's not marching. She told everybody at dinner that she can't stand in the hot sun or walk long distances in the heat anymore. I didn't really feel like eating my dessert after that. Somber. That's how I felt.

Somber: solemn in mood or extremely serious

Not a word I want to use too often but it wasn't all bad. How'd Nana put it? *There're other ways to contribute to the community.*

Maybe decisions like this will never be easy. That jolt

of electricity I felt over at the community center was real, but I miss the jolt I used to get from Jamila. Isn't there a way to have them both?

My phone buzzes and I'm almost afraid to look. Could it be Jamila . . . maybe?

"Hey, girl," says Michelle. "Ready for Sunday?"

It's nice that I can mention her name in our house again, but I want our talk to be private so I head out to the porch.

"Sunday is going to be great," she says. "My dad agrees with me that you should be on the front line. You; Clay; your grandfather, who, by the way, is very funny; and Mr. Charles. Multigenerational. That's what we're—"

"I'm not sure about all this."

There's a little gasp and a few seconds pass before Michelle says anything else.

"What do you mean?" Her voice gets quieter with each word. "I thought everything was all set."

"Yeah." I pause to take a deep breath so my voice stays strong. "I know how excited everybody is and I am too, but you didn't ask me how involved I wanted to be with the march. Nobody did."

Dead silence.

"Are you still there?" I ask.

"Where else would I be?" Michelle says with a deep sigh. "Why didn't you say something earlier?"

"You didn't give me a chance."

"Well, I just thought . . . after you met everybody at the meeting. I thought you'd . . ."

It doesn't feel good to hear Michelle struggling to explain herself so I help her out.

"I'm not mad or anything," I say. "The march is important, but I'm not comfortable with it right now." That's not the whole story but I don't want Michelle to know she's come between me and Jamila.

"Well," Michelle says, softening her voice. "I can't argue with that. You have to be comfortable with what you're doing. And look, you're right, I should have asked you about being out front. Sometimes I steamroll over people without really thinking about how I'm using my power."

"Your power?"

Michelle sighs. "You have it too. You just use it differently. You're more soft power."

"I wasn't trying to be powerful, Michelle. Just telling you what's on my mind."

"Call it whatever you want," she says. "It works."

Chapter Thirty-seven

EARNESTNESS

n. seriousness in intention, purpose, or effort: *Her earnestness was apparent by the tone of her voice.*

Dear Mama and Daddy,

Don't freak out because you're getting this email. I'm only doing it because you didn't answer the phone when I tried to call you. I'm not doing it because I'm mad.

Thank you for saying Clay and I can go to the march. I know it probably wasn't an easy decision since you're not here and can't really see everything that's going on. So please don't think I'm upset or anything when I say I may not go.

No, Mama, I'm not depressed, but thank you for asking Mrs. Mensah to check in on me. It's just that I need to get back together with Jamila, who broke her foot and her ankle and is mad at me because of a bunch of stuff that happened. Mainly, she thinks I'm choosing Michelle over her. That's not true but that's how she feels. Like she's been abandoned. I know that's not a good feeling because that's how I felt at the beginning of the summer.

So far this sounds like a "disturbing message" and, Daddy, I know how you feel about that, but keep reading. It isn't.

I spent the whole night thinking about all this and I'm going to use all my power to make Jamila happy on Sunday. I know a way to do that and to do what Nana says is important, to contribute to the community, at the same time.

I send this message to Mama and Daddy first thing Saturday morning. Mama responds right away.

I trust you to do the right thing, Neva. You'll know what that is.

Chapter Thirty-Eight

LOVE

n. 1. an intense feeling of deep affection *2.* a great interest and pleasure in something: *We share a love of music. 3.* a person or thing that one loves

I'm sitting on our back steps with my dictionary in my lap admiring all the pretty things in our yard. The blue spruce that separates Mr. Charles's house from ours, the little purple blossoms on their slender green stems in Nana's lavender patch, the bright red geraniums in the clay pot on the picnic table. I need these things to help me find the right words to tell Jamila how I feel about her. Words that will make her smile like she did when her daddy tickled her.

Most folks don't read the dictionary but I do. I thumb through the pages hoping my eyes will land on the magic words. But they're not here. Maybe I won't find the words I need in a dictionary. Well, what about the song I sang to Mama? Um . . . no. Those words aren't right either.

My mind keeps going back to how Jamila looked in her daddy's arms. Her *paapa*. Joyful . . . with her *paapa* . . . That's it. Maybe it's not English words I need. The way to Jamila's heart is through Twi, her daddy's language.

I race back into the house and up to my room to put my dictionary back in its place and grab my phone to search for Twi phrases. A bunch of language videos pop up, and lucky for me how to say "I love you" is not hard to find. I just hope these words are right 'cause I'm sure going to look bad if they're not.

Mafe wo *(I've missed you)*

I send the message to Jamila and sit on my bed, cross-legged, hoping for an answer.

Saa? Me nso mafe wo

It takes me a few minutes to translate what she wrote.

(Really? I've missed you too)

She's missed me too? I jump up and prance around my room before sending her another phrase.

Mehia wo *(I need you)*

Jamila types back.

212

Me nso mehia wo *(I also need you)*

I respond as soon as I've had a minute to translate.

Medɔ wo *(I love you)* I'll be right over!!!!! ♥

I tear out of my room and fly down the front stairs with one hand on the banister and my other hand on the wall. The Twi word for love has a letter I never saw before, ɔ. It looks like an inverted *c*. I jump down the last three stairs in one leap, wondering how you pronounce it. With an *aw* sound?

"Where's the fire?" asks Granddad. He's got stains on his T-shirt and this time they just may be from cooking.

"Jamila misses me." I grab a bagel from the platter in the center of the table. "Can I go see her?"

"Don't you think it's too—" Granddad starts to say, but Nana gives him a look. She can probably tell it would be too hard for me to sit still at the table.

I grab a handful of raspberries on my way through the garden and pop one in my mouth to make sure they're still ripe. The juice explodes in my mouth like fireworks.

Chapter Thirty-Nine

ANTICIPATION

n. the action of anticipating something; expectation or prediction: *Her eyes sparkled with anticipation.*

I'm not bragging on myself but texting Jamila in Twi was a great idea. Not just great. It was, what? I search through my brain for the best word I can think of. *Stupendous.* That's it.

Stupendous: extremely impressive

I know because Jamila's mama mouths a silent *thank you* when I step into their backyard.

"I didn't know you were a budding linguist," Mr. Mensah says, stepping back from his canvas.

"Your alphabet has some letters we don't have in English," I say, suppressing a grin and turning to look at his painting. It's a new one of his home country. This one has Jamila right in the middle of it.

"Just wait until you see it, ooh. We're bringing Mother Ghana to us since we cannot go to Her." Mr. Mensah gazes at his painting for a few seconds and smiles. "Yes, Twi and English both have the vowels *a*, *e*, *i*, *o*, and *u*, but Twi has two more vowels: *ɜ* and *ɔ*. *ɜ* sounds like *eh*, and *ɔ* sounds like *aw*.

"Maybe next year," says Mrs. Mensah, getting up from her chair and offering it to me. "Another year will give us more time to dream about it."

"Anticipation," I say.

"Yes," she says, smiling. "One of my favorite things."

Jamila sits at the little café table with her cast leg up on a chair just like the other day, but she breaks into a grin when I hand her the fruit I brought from our garden.

"You still have raspberries?" she says. "Clay hasn't eaten them all?"

"I saved these for you," I fib, but I know it's okay.

Jamila pops a few raspberries into her mouth and her eyes light up. She fakes a big swoon and clutches her neck like there's a big choker there or something. "Divine," she says, grinning. "That's something you would say."

"Come inside," Mrs. Mensah says, laughing and

gesturing to her husband. "Let's give them a chance to catch up."

Jamila and I are quiet for a few seconds before she brings up the subject we're both a little afraid to talk about.

"So, you're going to march tomorrow?"

"No . . . everything got sort of complicated so I decided not to."

"Won't Michelle miss you?"

"Maybe." I shrug. "But we're not really that close. Not like us."

Jamila lowers her head but I can still see the dimple in her right cheek.

"Well, everybody says she's doing good stuff. My *paapa* was talking about her last night."

"In a nice way, I hope." Jamila frowns and I tell her how Granddad and Nana didn't like Michelle at first.

"She's not bad," she says. "She just has a different style, that's all. And, you know, I've been wondering about all the political stuff. Everything that's going on around here."

"Me too," I say. "The meeting I went to was something."

I tell Jamila about the feeling of electricity that jumped from person to person.

"You're sure you want to miss that?"

"I don't know," I say, shrugging and looking down at my feet.

"Better think about it some more," she says. "I mean, I would go if I could."

"I don't know. I don't understand everything like Michelle—"

"I can't believe what I'm hearing," says Jamila, opening her eyes real wide. "Do what you always do." She sits up straight in her chair and pantomimes paging through an imaginary dictionary. "Look it up."

"I hope I don't look like that," I say, laughing along with her.

She licks her index finger and turns a few more imaginary pages.

"For real, girl. This is you."

Chapter Forty

ALIVE

adj. 1. having life, living, existing *2.* full of energy and spirit; lively: *Grandma's more alive than many people half her age.*

The March for Justice begins at twelve noon but Clay's been jumping around our house since eight this morning. He has the day off from the swim club but I think he should maybe do a few laps in the pool just to calm down.

Michelle took Clay's advice and replaced me with Anton on the front line, which is a very smart move if you ask me. She didn't, but that's okay. I have my own special plan for today.

"We should all stay together," says Granddad. "Clay, Anton, no messing around. You hear me?"

I slip out of the living room and sit on the porch in the rattan love seat with Nana. She has her eyes closed but her face tells me she's enjoying the fragrances wafting up from the garden when Mr. Mensah's Volvo pulls up in front of our house. Right on time.

Mr. Mensah gets out and hurries around the car to open the curbside door for Jamila. Her cast is the thing that pops out first, painted with Ghanaian and American flags. She leans out of the car and waves before wrapping her arms around her daddy's neck so he can lift her out of the car.

"Sorry I can't get in the dirt today," she says to Nana. She's followed out of the car by the rest of the Mensah family—her mama, holding her baby brother, and her auntie.

That's Mr. Charles's cue to retrieve the supplies we hid at his house yesterday night. A big aluminum tub, ice, bottles of water, and lots and lots of iced tea. It was Mr. Mensah's idea to chill the tea in red, gold, and green plastic pitchers. The colors of the Ghanaian flag.

Mr. Charles gets things set up just in time to hand bottles of water to five people walking down the street carrying signs but then I'm surprised by something Jamila's auntie does.

She clears her throat and stands right next to me. "My brother has told me something very nice about you," she says, nodding at Jamila's daddy. "We were all so sad that our trip had to be canceled but you found a way to bring us all together and, most importantly, to put a smile back on my niece's face."

"Oh, I almost forgot," says Mr. Mensah. He darts back to his car and pulls a boom box from the back seat. "Eh! Music!" he says, holding the box high over his head like he's crossing a river and doesn't want it to get wet. "We'll send the marchers off on just the right beat."

He turns the music on and the drums and horns of highlife send a jolt of electricity through every single one of us. It's hard not to move, but who would want to stand still?

Nana and Jamila sway together on the love seat and I feel the energy coming off them. Is this what Mama feels when she's onstage? I tap my feet and start to sway, soaking up all the good feelings swirling around our porch.

"Go ahead," says Mrs. Mensah, clapping her baby's hands together.

Mama said I'd know what to do and she was right. I throw my head back and let myself go all silly and loose and free.

"Baby Girl sure can dance," says Granddad.

"It's called prancing, Granddad," says Clay. "*P-R-A-N-C-I-N-G*."

Prancing: dancing or moving in a lively or spirited manner; capering

I step down from the porch and weave my way through our garden. My eyes land on the brilliant red raspberries hanging now in full clusters. I scoop up a handful as I glide along the paving stones to the sidewalk. My brother is the first one off the porch to join me.

WHAT THEY MEAN TO ME
By NEVA BEANE

My girl Jamila showed me how I look with my nose in a dictionary: a little bit nerdy, a little bit funny, a whole lot of just being who I am. Okay, I own it. Here are some of my favorite (and not-so-favorite) words. They're not in alphabetical order. I just went through my story from start to finish and pulled stuff out.

MY FAVORITE
(AND NOT-SO-FAVORITE)
WORDS

LINGERIE is women's fancy underwear and pajamas. From what I can tell, lingerie seems to be lacy and frilly and sort of expensive, but it's just another style of underwear. You know, like sports bras are a separate style.

TROLLEYS is short for trolley cars. We still have them in parts of West Philly. They're basically buses with an electric motor that draws power from overhead wires. They used to be a lot noisier than they are now. Instead of making a clanking sound, these days they sort of "whoosh" when they go by.

A **FRAGRANCE** is a perfume or aftershave. (Yes, guys use fragrances too.) I think everybody already has their own natural fragrance. That's enough for me.

NEWSY is a Philly thing. It means nosy or nosey, however you want to spell it. It's how you describe somebody who should mind their own business.

To **MARVEL** means to be filled with wonder or astonishment. For example, some people don't think clothes hanging outside to dry looks nice, but I marvel at how our jeans, and tops, and towels dance in the breeze when they're on the clothesline in our backyard. It's better for the environment when you don't use a dryer, and it makes the clothes smell really, really good.

CLOTHESPINS are wooden or plastic clips used to fasten clothes to a clothesline. And down in Center City, there's a forty-five-foot-tall steel sculpture of a giant clothespin across the street from City Hall. It's a Philly landmark.

MURALS, paintings on sides of buildings, are big in Philly too. I mean, Philly has thousands of them. They're called "wall art," and they look really cool.

EROSION is a process where the surface of the Earth gets worn down. It can be caused by things like wind and rain. Sinkholes are caused by water erosion.

A **CRISIS** can be any really bad or dramatic event. Of course, some crises are more important than others, but for me, not being able to get my ring unstuck from my hair was a crisis, especially when it happened in front of my friend's mama. So embarrassing.

Don't be surprised if you're asked to sign a **PETITION** at some point. It's usually a written request signed by a lot of folks asking people in charge of a certain situation for something. For example, you might want to petition your town to add a stop sign at a busy intersection.

A **DASHIKI** is a big, colorful, loose shirt, originally from West Africa.

SWITCHING is an old-school word. It refers to women walking in a show-offy kind of way. I asked Nana if there was a word for men walking to show off. Her answer: "strolling."

A **COMMOTION** is a big old confused mess. Think of a food fight in the school cafeteria. That's a commotion.

The **VESTIBULE** is the part of our house between the front door and the living room. It's like a short hallway that you can walk through in four or five steps.

DÉCOLLETAGE is a French word. At first I thought it just referred to a low neckline, but it describes a dress or blouse cut low in the back or across the shoulders too.

Clay wore a **TOGA** when he was in a play about ancient Rome. A toga is a loose piece of cloth that a man wears over a tunic. It covers the whole body except the right arm. You probably won't see anybody wearing one these days unless they're in a movie or something.

A **REBEL** is a person who resists authority, control, or tradition. There are lots of ways to stand up for what's important to you. One is to write and circulate a petition.

It's not always bad to be **HARDHEADED**. It means to be practical and realistic.

Here's another Philly thing: We love **WATER ICE** in the summertime. It's frozen and made from water, sugar, and fruit flavoring. It's close to sorbet but softer.

A **STILETTO** is a kind of woman's shoe with a thin, really high heel.

It's not nice to call somebody a **LIGHTWEIGHT**. It means they're not important or don't know their stuff.

WHAT YOU NO GOOD? One of Granddad's sayings. It means "what have you been up to?"

MIGRAINE. This is my least favorite word in the entire world. A migraine is a really bad headache. Not only does your head throb like a marching band is performing inside it, but when I get a migraine, I also can't stand light or the smell of food. And sometimes the headache can last for more than one day. Not fun.

A **SERENADE** is music or a song usually played outside under the window of someone you love. Okay, I serenaded Mama by phone, but that's only because she was so far away.

LINGUIST. This is probably what I should be when I grow up. A linguist studies the structure, use, and psychology of language. Some linguists speak many languages and work as language teachers or as interpreters at the United Nations. But linguists also study things like how languages change over time and how language is learned by children.

So, we end with my best friend, Jamila, doing a **PANTOMIME** of me. A pantomime is an exaggerated gesture that shows an action or an emotion without using words. You know how clowns pantomime crying? Exactly!

Acknowledgments

This book would not have come into being without the inspiration from my brothers. They helped shape the seed of the story without even knowing it. I'm also grateful to my rock star literary family, editor Andrea Davis Pinkney and agent Miriam Altshuler, who kept me on the path.

There are also friends who provided much needed support, Steve Sadoski and especially Zusong Tindana.

And above all else, my husband, Rob, who has always believed in me.

About the Author

Christine Kendall's short fiction has appeared in numerous literary journals. Her debut novel, *Riding Chance*, was nominated for an NAACP Image Award in the category of Outstanding Literary Work for Youth/Teens. Christine lives in Philadelphia, PA, where she cocurates and hosts the award-winning reading series, Creative at the Cannery.